'Be your age!'

'And what age is that?' asked a voice from the doorway—Dr Fordyce's voice, deep, pleasant and drawling with humour.

'Why, Doctor,' Poppy said, adding a little trill of laughter for effect, 'you know no gentleman should ever ask a lady that.'

'Who said that I was a gentleman?' asked the doctor, an innocent gleam in his eye.

'I rather took it for granted that you were,' said Poppy, and added silkily, 'but perhaps that was a mistake.'

Dear Reader

Margaret O'Neill has written a quartet based around Princes Park Hospital, and CHRISTMAS IS FOREVER launches the four books, which will appear in following months. Poppy works on the paediatric ward, while Jennifer in SECOND THOUGHTS by Caroline Anderson works in Paediatric Outpatients, so plenty of babies and children this festive month! Animals, too, in CELEBRITY VET by Carol Wood, finishing with a Scottish island cottage hospital in CURE FOR HEARTACHE by Patricia Robertson. All home-grown stories to wish you a very merry Christmas.

The Editor

Margaret O'Neill started scribbling at four and began nursing at twenty. She contracted TB, and, when recovered, did her British Tuberculosis Association nursing training before general training at the Royal Portsmouth Hospital. She married, had two children, and, with her late husband, she owned and managed several nursing homes. Now retired and living in Sussex, she still has many nursing contacts. Her husband would have been delighted to see her books in print.

Recent titles by the same author:

SEEDS OF LOVE
HANDFUL OF DREAMS

CHRISTMAS IS FOREVER

BY
MARGARET O'NEILL

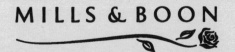

MILLS & BOON

MILLS & BOON LIMITED
ETON HOUSE, 18–24 PARADISE ROAD
RICHMOND, SURREY, TW9 1SR

First published in Great Britain 1993
by Mills & Boon Limited

© Margaret O'Neill 1993

Australian copyright 1993
Philippine copyright 1993
This edition 1993

ISBN 0 263 78379 0

Set in 10 on 12 pt Linotron Times
03-9312-51633

Typeset in Great Britain by Centracet, Cambridge
Made and printed in Great Britain

CHAPTER ONE

'Poppy, Sister wants you in her office.' The third-year student gave Poppy a sympathetic smile. 'She looks pretty riled up.'

'Oh, lord, now what am I supposed to have done?'

'No idea, but you'd better get going; I don't think patience is in her vocabulary this morning.'

'Oh, well, here goes.' Automatically Poppy smoothed down her apron and put up a hand to make sure that her cap was straight on her short corn-coloured hair, as she made for the ward office.

She knocked at the glass door.

'Sister, you wanted to see me?'

'Have you asked to be moved off this ward, Staff Nurse Pope?'

'No, Sister.'

Sister Taylor made a grumbling, indistinct noise in her throat and gave Poppy a sharp look. 'Well, the powers that be have decided that they want you on Peter Pan, as from tomorrow, on a maternity leave replacement. You're to report to the office after lunch for further instructions.'

'Peter Pan?' Poppy's normally low-key voice almost squeaked.

Sister Taylor gave her a sour look. 'Yes, Staff Nurse, on the paediatric unit. How do you feel about that?'

Poppy wanted to say, Over the moon, but realised that this wouldn't be too well received by the dedicated sister on Men's Medical. 'I'm happy to go anywhere that I'm sent, Sister. Every ward has something to offer, and I've been doing relief now for two years, so I am quite used to zipping from one ward to another.'

'"Zipping"—is that what you call it? Well, at least you're doing it here at Princes Park in your own training hospital. I've heard that some student nurses nowadays don't get offered a job in their own hospital at all, not even in relief capacity. They have to move elsewhere directly they qualify, and that I think is very sad.' Her rather severe face relaxed into the semblance of a smile. 'I feel sorry for you young nurses, I really do. Life seems so much easier in many ways—you have the sort of freedom that was only a dream to my generation of nurses—but you don't have the security that we had, or the closely knit feeling of family that kept us going when the going was very tough.'

Poppy nearly said that that was what her father said, but bit back the remark in time. Sister Taylor, together with most of the staff, wouldn't know that Professor Sir Rowland Pope, famous in medical circles as an eminent paediatric consultant, was her father. She had guarded that secret ever since she had started her training. She had no intention of climbing the nursing ladder via her father's position, and had resisted steadily.

'But Poppy,' he'd said, sounding quite exasperated, 'it's not nepotism, or favouritism, or any other "ism". Nesta Cooper is desperate for a first-year staff nurse. Her current one leaves in a month's time.'

'Oh, come on, Daddy, St Christopher's only has to advertise and you'll have nurses queuing down the street for the chance to work there.'

Her father said drily, 'It is quality we look for at St Christopher's, you know, not quantity.'

'And how do you know that I'm quality, Pa, that I'll measure up to your astronomical standards? You've never seen me at work.'

Sir Rowland had looked pained. 'Oh, really, Poppy, now you're being silly. You didn't get the gold for your inter-hospital exams for nothing, and I have made a few, very discreet, enquiries over the years.' Poppy scowled, and he held up his hand to prevent her from interrupting. 'Any father would do that much, my dear girl, so don't read anything into it. You know that I've always respected your desire to make it on your own. I just think that now that you're trained you might be a little less adamant about what you see as my attempt to help.'

Poppy gave her father a hug. 'Yes, you've been great about it, Daddy, darling, but I want to press on under my own steam. Believe me, I'll come running to you if things get desperate.'

'Promise?'

'Promise.'

And there had been times over the last two years, Poppy reflected as she sped back to the ward from Sister's office, when she'd almost begged her father to help her find a paediatric post. Her own hospital, Princes Park, simply hadn't had a vacancy on the children's unit in all that time, and nothing had come of any of the advertisements that she had answered. Paediatric nursing was either overstaffed or hospitals were economising. She could have taken other staff posts on a permanent basis and started climbing the professional ladder, but her heart was set on specialis-

ing in children's nursing, and she had waited patiently.
Now it looked as if her patience was going to pay
dividends. Relieving somebody on maternity leave
meant three, perhaps six months on paediatrics, time
enough to gain experience and apply for a post
demanding just that.

She hummed cheerfully as she joined the first-year
student at the medicine trolley.

'You seem jolly happy, Staff,' said the student. 'Had
some good news?'

'The best ever, Lucy, news that I've been waiting
for for yonks.'

Lucy looked at her expectantly, but Poppy had no
intention of telling the young student about her good
fortune until she had told her father and her two
closest friends, Ruth and Jacky. 'Secret,' she said, and
grinned at the girl as she unlocked the mobile drugs
cupboard and made herself concentrate. 'Come along,
then, Nurse, let's get this show on the road. Who have
we first?'

'John Baker.'

'And what's Mr Baker's diagnosis?'

'Stomach trouble, probably a gastric ulcer, and he's
in for investigation.'

'Good, and what does this medicine do?' She held
up the plastic beaker with chalky white fluid in it.

'It's an antacid, Staff, which neutralises the stomach
contents and relieves the pain caused by the acidity.'

'Spot-on. Now take that to the patient and make
sure that he drinks it all.'

The medicine round continued, followed by the
dressings round, then ward lunches, until at one
o'clock Sister told Poppy to go to lunch herself, and

then check with the office before visiting Peter Pan to
find out what duties she would be on the following
day.

She was in the admin office before one-thirty, eager to
confirm her relief appointment to the paediatric unit.

'How long will I be on the unit?' she asked the
admin officer.

'Probably for three to four months, provided that
the unit sister and the medical staff approve. Go and
report to Sister O'Brien.'

'Oh, that's great,' said Poppy with a huge smile.
'Peter Pan, here I come.'

Sister Rose O'Brien was a round, dumpy little lady in
her late forties. She had reddish hair, piled high on
her head with her frilly sister's cap perched on top,
blazing blue eyes, and, legend had it, a temper to
match both hair and eyes when roused. This was rare,
though, and only occurred when 'her children' were in
any way threatened. The children adored her and so
did most of the staff. Poppy had known her three years
before when she did her training stint on the ward.
Working there then had confirmed her desire to
specialise in paediatrics.

Sister was sitting at her desk in her office, talking to
someone who had his back to the door, when Poppy
arrived to find out what her duties would be the
following day.

She greeted Poppy warmly. 'So you've managed to
get back to us at last, my dear. Do you still want to do
children's?'

'I do, Sister, I've never stopped wanting to. I just

haven't had the chance. Fancy you remembering me after all this time.'

'I always remember my good students, the really keen ones. Now come on in and meet your future boss and colleagues, while we sort out the roster.'

Poppy gave a pleased smile at the compliment. She stepped further into the room and Sister's visitor stood up and turned round to greet her. He was tall and lean, and didn't so much stand up as uncoil, she thought, as he loomed over her. His face was long and narrow, a handsome face, with a shock of dark hair springing from his high forehead. His eyes were dark brown, and a well marked mouth quirked at the corners above a strong jaw, and beneath a straight, rather patrician nose. Black eyebrows arched over his dark eyes. A rather formidable face, thought Poppy as she held out her hand, but a face to be trusted.

Sister O'Brien was saying, as, head bent, she riffled through some papers looking for the duty sheet, 'Nick, meet Poppy—Penelope Pope. Poppy, this is Dr Nicholas Fordyce; he joined us a few weeks ago, as senior registrar.'

Poppy smiled up at the doctor as her hand slipped into his, and then she lowered her eyes and gaped at the forest of badges, emblems and pictures that decorated his white coat. In fact, there was very little coat to be seen. From hem to shoulder it was covered with stuck-on colours and pictures. Somewhere around his left lapel was a large round blob of a badge, with 'Doctor Nick' written on it in large print.

In the three years that had passed since Poppy was on the ward, Sister O'Brien had certainly introduced more radical changes. She'd always been hell-bent on making things as unfrightening for the kids coming into hospital as possible, but in those days it had stopped short with the nursing staff, who wore flowered aprons instead of white starched ones, and a few cartoon pictures displayed round the ward. Now everything was vibrant with colour, apparently, including the medical staff.

She raised her eyes again to meet the doctor's. It was going to be great working with Sister O'Brien and this good-looking man, who wasn't afraid to don a silly coat to reassure the children. It was a shock to find that his mouth no longer held the hint of a smile, and that he was frowning at her with evident displeasure.

'Staff Nurse Pope,' he said, peering at her, his dark eyes expressionless. 'Penelope Pope?' he said in a questioning voice, as if he couldn't quite believe it.

'Yes, for my sins.' She tried to inject a cheerful, throw-away note into her voice, but the look on Nicholas Fordyce's face chilled her words. His mouth had set into a straight line; his dark eyes had gone hard and as glazed as marbles. He dropped her hand and turned away from her abruptly. It was as if she had offended him, but how? What had she said or done in those few moments that he could possibly take objection to?

Sister O'Brien finished scrabbling among the papers on her desk and waved the duty roster over her head. 'Eureka! Now let's see, Poppy, you are replacing Janice Walters, who is going off to have her baby, lucky girl. She's working till the end of the week. She had planned to stay on till after Christmas, but has been advised to stop work now as her blood-pressure is rather high. I want you to do as much as you can to relieve her over the next few days, as well as learning the ropes. You're on an eight to five tomorrow, OK?'

Poppy nodded and smiled. 'That's great, Sister, I'll be here bright and early.'

'Welcome aboard, you couldn't come at a better time than Christmas on Peter Pan. Believe me, you'll have your best Christmas ever in hospital.'

'I know I will, Sister. I can't tell you how much I'm looking forward to working with the children.'

And she was, she told herself as she made her way back to Men's Medical, in spite of Dr Nicholas Fordyce giving her the cold shoulder. Why had he done that, and what had happened in the few moments after he'd turned round to replace his quirky smile with an uncompromising frown? He'd repeated her name in a strange sort of way after Sister O'Brien had introduced them, and stared at her as if he couldn't believe what he was seeing. What was there about her looks that had caused the doctor such consternation, to change him from being pleasant to being angry? Thank goodness that Sister O'Brien hadn't noticed anything. The admin sister had said that she would be on Peter Pan for several months, provided that both the ward sister and the medical staff were satisfied with her. It was hardly a brilliant start when even before she had begun work she'd inadvertently annoyed the new registrar.

She dashed into the staff cloakroom before reporting back on duty, and checked herself in the mirror. What was there about her that Dr Fordyce hadn't liked? She stared at her reflection. Nothing had changed; the samed fine-boned features were there, with the determined chin, the same mouth, always on the point of smiling, except when she was in an obstinate mood, and the same hazel-green eyes and short mop of honey-coloured hair. All were in place and looking as usual. Whatever it was that had bothered Dr Fordyce wasn't obvious. Poppy shrugged. 'The man must be mad,' she told her mirror image. 'Perhaps he just doesn't like honey-coloured blondes. Anyway, neither he nor anyone else is going to spoil Peter Pan for me, and I'll make damned sure that I don't do anything to offend the touchy Dr Fordyce.'

Her friends Ruth Knight and Jacky Forbes were thrilled for her when they heard the news.

'We must have a party and celebrate,' they said in unison.

They and Poppy shared accommodation in a hospital-owned house in the market town of Princes Hollow.

They were great friends, but couldn't understand why she was reluctant to take up a permanent staff nursing post while waiting for paediatrics. They understood that she didn't want to be diverted from her goal by becoming interested in another discipline, but had recently persuaded her that it was time to think again after waiting for two years, and had suggested a deadline till the New Year.

Now they were thrilled for her that the opportunity to work on Peter Pan had occurred just before she reached the deadline, and she could achieve her ambition.

'It's fate,' said Ruth, 'you being sent to kids just before your two years are up.'

'Yep,' said Jacky, beaming from ear to ear, pleased as punch for her friend. 'It's super. Now, about this party, when shall we have it? I'm off on Saturday and Sunday this week; what about you two?'

'Off Sunday,' said Ruth. 'So either day would suit me fine.'

'I'm on all the weekend,' said Poppy, 'but I've got Monday off.'

'Right,' said Jacky. 'Sunday evening, then. I'll have the weekend to get things ready, and Ruth can help on Sunday, and you, dear Poppy, can do all the clearing-up on Monday, when we stagger, exhausted and hung-over, to work. How about that?'

'Sounds brilliant,' agreed Poppy.

'Let's spread the word,' said Ruth. 'I'll start ringing around; you two sort out the food.'

'Have you told your father yet?' asked Jacky.

'No, I tried to phone him earlier, but he wasn't in, so I left a message on his answer machine, telling him that I had some news to pass on. Depends when he gets home whether he rings back.'

'He'll be thrilled for you.'

'Yes,' said Poppy, beaming. 'He certainly will.'

Ruth did some telephoning. 'I've been in touch with a load of people,' she announced. 'And they're going to let everyone else know about Sunday.'

'For goodness' sake — how many people are you talking about coming?' asked Poppy.

'Oh, thirty, forty, something like that,' Ruth said airily.

'You've got to be joking,' said Poppy. 'I thought you meant just friends, not half the blessed hospital.'

'So, you've got a lot of friends, and you're a popular lady,' replied Ruth with a grin. 'Oh, come on, Poppy, it is nearly Christmas; you wouldn't deny anyone the chance of a party to wish you well, would you?'

'No way, it's just a bigger celebration than I'd thought to have.'

'Well, who's a lucky girl, then?'

Poppy was on duty at a quarter to eight the following morning.

'You're an early bird,' said the night staff nurse, whizzing round Peter Pan doing a last-minute check before handing over.

'I've waited ages to get on to peds; getting in ten minutes early is no big deal. Can I do anything to help?'

'Check the feed room,' suggested the staff nurse. 'Make sure all the bottles are cleaned and sterilised, and everything's prepared for the next feed list. Check off the list with the junior.'

'Sure, will do.'

The junior gave her a warm welcome. 'Oh, Staff, have you come to help me with the specials?'

'I have. Now where have you got to?'

'Baby Black — Formula Five, all mixed; can you bottle it for me, please, and put it in the rack?'

'Baby Clark — MEM; that's in the marked jug there.'

'When I first worked here during my last year of training,' said Poppy, 'I remember wondering what the hell MEM meant. Everything else was plain formula this and formula that, but MEM. . .?'

'Yes, I was the same. It seems so obvious when you know — Mother's Expressed Milk — but it's like a clue in a crossword when you first see it.'

They worked in silence for another few minutes, completing the half a dozen bottles of special feeds for the babies. There were only the six cubicle babies at the moment, all two weeks to nine months. Younger babies were kept in the separate special baby unit. Nine-month-plus babies were moved out of the glass cubicles into the infant cots at one end of Peter Pan ward.

That process hadn't changed since she was last on the ward, but other things had, she discovered as she worked her way through her action list during the course of the morning. Nurses still wore caps, but they were decorated like party hats with badges and emblems, just like Dr Nick's white coat, thought Poppy, smiling as she remembered her first sight of him yesterday.

She scooped up the two-year-old Angella from the floor, where she sat surrounded by bricks, just managing to catch her as she shuffled speedily off on her tiny bottom to evade Poppy, apparently quite unaffected by the splints that held her congenitally deformed little legs in position.

'Bath for you, my girl,' said Poppy, waltzing the child round in her arms, so that she shouted with delight. 'Dance, dance. . .' sang Poppy, and whirled round to come face to face with Dr Fordyce. 'Oh,' she said. 'Oh, I'm sorry.'

'Why sorry?' The doctor beamed at Angella and chucked her under the chin. 'And how's my little angel this morning?'

'Thoctor Nick, Thoctor Nick,' crowed the child, and held her arms out to him. 'Thance, thance,' she cried, her slight speech impediment sounding delightful and inviting as it turned her 'd's into 'th's.

Nick Fordyce took her into his arms and swung her round as Poppy had done. 'Dance with you, little lady?' he said with a smile. 'It'll be a pleasure.' He turned to look at Poppy, the smile gone, a neutral expression on his face. 'And where were you heading for, Staff?' he asked formally.

'To the bathroom; madam here has an appointment with the bathtub.'

'And some exercises?'

'Just as you prescribed: splints off, and a little gentle exercise in the water, Doctor.'

'Good,' he said briskly. 'What I want to do is to prepare this young woman for the hydrotherapy pool. The chances are that she'll take to it without any problems, but one can never be sure with small children; a larger expanse of water can be frightening for them.'

'Yes, I can see how that might be so if they haven't been used to going to swimming-baths, or the seaside.'

'And this little one hasn't. I've established that neither of her parents swim, so seeing even the small children's pool might be quite frightening for Angella, and yet free exercise in the pool could be such a help to her.'

'I'll see what I can do to make bathtime funtime,' said Poppy.

'Yes, I'm sure you will,' said Dr Nick gruffly. 'But then I suppose that looking after kids is kids' stuff to you, with your antecedents.'

He didn't wait for an astonished Poppy to reply, but just tickled a delighted Angella and handed her back into Poppy's waiting arms. 'There we go, poppet,' he said, 'back to Nurse.' And he strode away down the ward.

'Now whatever did he mean by that?' Poppy asked Angella, who looked at her with huge, uncomprehending eyes. 'Not that it matters,' she muttered, 'what the good doctor thinks, as long as he doesn't dislike me enough to get me moved off the ward. I'll just have to bear his snide remarks.'

Ignoring the small baths that stood against the walls, she filled one of the large baths that stood on raised plinths in the middle of the bathroom. This would enable Angella to exercise her legs as per Dr Nick's instructions. It would be interesting to see how her small patient took to the large plastic tub, bigger in circumference, shallower than a normal domestic bath, but deep enough to contain enough water to support the small limbs. It was a splendid halfway measure to introduce her to the therapy pool in the rehabilitation unit that she would soon be going to daily.

Angella loved her bath, and was quite unafraid of the volume of water. She splashed and screamed with delight as Poppy, supporting her with one arm, helped her to straighten her small legs by trying to trap a plastic ball between her thighs, and then between her ankles.

Two other nurses, one a junior sister, the other a third-year student, with their small charges in tow, came into the bathroom and started baths. Poppy had met them both briefly over the years. The junior sister, Diana Jacobs, had been a staff nurse like herself when Poppy had worked on Paediatrics as a student nearly three years ago; now she was assistant to Sister Rose O'Brien.

'How's it going?' she asked Poppy. 'Settling in on your first morning?'

'It's great, I'm loving it. I'm grateful to Janice for getting pregnant.'

'Yes, I hope that she's going to be all right,' said Diana. 'Her BP's very high at times; that's why she didn't come in first thing this morning. Rose thinks that she ought to stop at once now that you're here, and not try to work for the rest of the week.'

'I suppose it would be sensible of her to do so.'

'Yes, but she's hating the idea of not working from now till the baby's due. I'll bet she'll be popping in and out all the time. Peter Pan has that effect on people.'

'Sister won't mind that?'

'Not a bit. Rosie O'Brien's a darling, and loves her staff almost as much as her children; we're all part of her family.'

Poppy removed a reluctant Angella from the bath.

'Come on, poppet,' she said. 'You've had enough for one day.' She gave her full attention to the little girl, drying and powdering her, and re-splinting her legs, teasing her gently as she worked. 'There, sweetheart, you're all done and smelling gorgeous.' She buried her face in the child's soft neck beneath her black curls and kissed her gently, and then looked across at Diana. 'And what about the new reg, Dr Fordyce; does he mind people, even old staff, wandering in and out of the ward willy-nilly?'

'Nick Fordyce? No, of course he doesn't mind; he's super. He's a stickler for work, and everything's got to be spot-on for the kids, but in fact he welcomes visitors to the ward as long as they're a help not a hindrance. He says that it's more natural for children to have people coming in and out, more homely.'

Poppy looked at Diana a little uncertainly. Should she say anything about the doctor's strange reaction towards her, or should she keep that rather odd little incident to herself? She decided against confiding in her colleague; obviously Dr Fordyce was highly thought of by Diana, and, from all that she had heard, by the rest of the staff.

'Oh, he sounds like good news,' she said rather lamely. 'I'm sure that I'm going to enjoy working for him.'

'Well, if you don't, you'll be the only nurse who doesn't,' said Diana. 'There is just one thing that he might be touchy about where you're concerned, but I'm sure that it won't last.'

'What on earth can that be? I don't even know the man.'

'Don't get uptight about it, for heaven's sake, but he's rather keen on Nina Caldwell; they've been going about together since he came to Princes. I think she rather hoped to relieve Janice for her maternity leave.'

'Nina? But I didn't think that she was especially keen on paediatrics?'

'She's certainly keen on our paediatric registrar, so perhaps it amounts to the same thing.'

'You mean that he might resent me for getting the job?'

'I can't see it really, he doesn't seem that sort of a chap, but you never know. Not that he'd do anything to jeopardise the kids, so as long as you do your damnedest for them he'll be OK. Just watch your step and don't put a foot wrong, and you'll have Dr Nick eating out of your hand.'

'To be forewarned,' said Poppy cheerfully, 'is to be forearmed. The good doctor will be pole-axed by my efficiency.'

She laughed, gathered up a gurgling, happy Angella, and returned to the play-room.

By the end of her first day on Peter Pan, Poppy was tired but elated. It had been a breathless sort of day, getting to know all the children on the ward. There were the baby cubicles, divided by a glassed-in corridor from the main general ward, the oncology wing of six beds for children suffering from cancer conditions, and another wing for VICs, or very ill children, not fit enough for the hurly-burly of the general ward. Even the general ward was partly subdivided to accommodate the infants up to eighteen months, separating them from the bigger children, and a small section of screened recovery beds, where children returning from operations were nursed for a day or so.

The centre of the Peter Pan unit was the play-room. Here, children who were fit enough spent their days playing with each other and learning through play to recover from their illnesses or injuries, or in some cases to come to terms with their chronic conditions. There were Down's syndrome children and spina bifida infants, and children with various deformities, besides those admitted for acute conditions to be treated by surgery or medication. Their boisterous good spirits were the most inspiring thing about the ward and the small patients. Very few of them remained dull and depressed for long, whatever their illness, responding to the cheerful atmosphere around them.

Like everything else at Princes, thought Poppy, the paediatric unit was well planned and superbly managed.

There was only one fly in the ointment as far as she could see, and that was Dr Nicholas Fordyce, and his strange attitude towards her. Why he was so abrupt with her she had no idea. He had a reputation for being friendly with everyone, and was adored by the children. Well, maybe yesterday she had caught him at a bad moment — and today, she was forced to ask herself, when she had been playing with Angella and he had looked at her so coldly, what reason had there been for that? She didn't know, and wondered if perhaps she had imagined it.

She made her way through the car park to where she had left her Mini, and shrugged off the memory of the paediatric registrar and his reaction to her. She cheered herself with the thought that they might at least work together amicably, even if they never became very friendly. She was not going to let anything deter her from doing her level best to make this Christmas on Peter Pan the best ever, and to hell with Dr Fordyce.

It was a bitterly cold night, frosty although it was only just after five o'clock, with a black velvet sky full of glittering stars and the ground underfoot already icy. A typical early December night, with Christmas just around the corner, thought Poppy, struggling to push her key into the car-door lock. A night to gorge on tea and toast, and chat with her friends.

'If only,' she said out loud to the empty car park, 'I can get the damned door open.'

'Having trouble?' asked a voice.

The voice, though it sounded vaguely familiar, made Poppy jump. The car park was well lit, but she hadn't seen anybody about a moment before. It was as if someone had been deliberately hiding, and the thought was quite frightening. There had been reports of prowlers around; could this be one of them? She shivered, partly with cold, and partly with a quiver of fear, and peered across the tops of the intervening cars. She still couldn't see anybody, as there was a Range Rover blocking her view.

'Who is it?' she called.

'Nick Fordyce,' said the voice, and she heard foot-steps coming round the parked cars, and she recog-nised the doctor clearly as he came into view from behind the Range Rover. 'Oh,' he said, sounding surprised. 'It's you, Staff Nurse Pope.'

'Yes,' breathed Poppy, torn between relief at finding that it was not a stranger, and annoyance at discover-ing who it was. 'I thought you might be a prowler.'

'Well, I'm not,' said the doctor, sounding irritated. 'Why can't you get your car door open?'

'I — I think it's iced up.' Her teeth were chattering now, with a combination of fright and cold. 'I wish to God you'd said who you were when you first spoke; you gave me one hell of a fright.'

'Sorry, Staff, I'm sure,' said Nick sarcastically. 'I'm surprised that you frighten so easily.'

'What do you mean by that, Dr Fordyce? Any woman might have been scared in the circumstances — a dark night, no one about.'

Dr Fordyce shrugged. 'I don't know, I just had the feeling that you were a tough superwoman type who could and would demolish any opposition, male or female.'

'Well, I certainly wouldn't let anyone walk all over me, but I'm as vulnerable as the next woman when it comes to meeting strangers on a dark night. And now, if you don't mind, I must try and get this de-iced.' She bent down and blew on the iced-up keyhole.

'You'll never get anywhere like that; it's been freezing all afternoon.'

'Have you any other suggestions?' asked Poppy, her voice as freezing as the weather.

'Two,' said the doctor.

'And are you going to let me into the secret before I freeze to death?'

'One, I can give you a lift to wherever you're going, or, two, I can get the de-icer spray from my car, and work a minor miracle.' He was grinning mockingly, seemingly well aware of her badly concealed fury that it should be he who had come to her aid. 'Well, what is it to be — one or two?'

'Number two, please,' said Poppy in a flat voice. 'I suppose you sprayed your car with de-icer before you left it.'

'That's right,' replied the doctor. 'As the sort of sensible precaution that you might take in the future.'

'Oh, I will, never fear,' said Poppy firmly. 'I won't risk this happening to me again, ever.'

'Sensible girl,' he said, in what she took to be such a patronising manner that she almost choked. 'I'll fetch it; don't go away.'

Poppy fumed; as if she could or would go anywhere.

She knew that he was winding her up, but couldn't somehow prevent herself from saying the wrong thing.

'If you're sure that it is not too much trouble,' she said sweetly, sarcastically.

'No trouble,' said Nicholas Fordyce expansively, 'especially for. . .'

'For?'

'It doesn't matter; forget it.'

What had he been going to say? she wondered, when a few minutes later, after he had freed the lock, and she had thanked him with as much warmth that she could muster, she was able to drive away.

'Drive carefully,' he'd said, as she had moved off. 'It's slippery.'

His whole manner had been so odd. He had seemed to want to and yet resent the need to help her. It was almost as if two opposing factors were warring within him, which was ridiculous, since they hardly knew each other; there was nothing for them to war about.

CHAPTER TWO

RESOLUTELY Poppy shook her mind free of the doctor, and concentrated on driving carefully along the icy roads until she reached home. It wasn't true, Poppy thought, as she parked the car on the drive, what Sister Taylor or her father said about hospitals not producing such a feeling of 'family' as they had in the old days. She and her two closest friends, and most of those in the set with whom they had trained, felt very much a family unit, which continued to function wherever they worked after they had finished their training.

As if to emphasise this point, Ruth flung open the front door before Poppy had time to unlock it.

'You're late,' she said, as they walked through the warm hall to the large old-fashioned kitchen. 'You were off at five; where on earth have you been? I was quite worried about you driving home on these icy roads; apparently there have already been quite a few accidents, according to the local news.'

'Wow, what it is to be loved,' laughed Poppy. 'Sorry you were worried about me. I got stuck in the car park.'

'The car park?' Ruth placed a steaming mug of tea in front of Poppy.

'Yes, my key wouldn't go into the lock; it was all iced-up.' She took a sip of tea. 'Lovely,' she said, 'just what I needed.'

'How on earth did you manage to unfreeze it — get

some nice strong man to blow his nice hot breath on it?'

'Got my new registrar Dr Nicholas Fordyce to use his de-icer spray on it.'

'Oh,' said Ruth with a laugh. 'The white knight in shining armour to the rescue. Nice work, Staff Nurse Pope, there's nothing like capturing the interest of your registrar on your first day. You're sure that your lock was all iced-up?' she teased.

'Quite sure, and, before you get any more bright ideas about Nick Fordyce being a knight coming to the assistance of a maiden in distress, let me tell you that he was a very reluctant knight errant, and I was an even more reluctant maiden.'

'What do you mean — reluctant?'

'Well, that's just it, it's hard to explain. Look, let me just get changed and then I'll tell you while we're having supper all about the charismatic — only not with me — Nick Fordyce. By the way, what is for supper? I'm starving.'

'Well, you know me, I'm a woman of limited expertise in the kitchen, unlike you and Jacky, but tonight we have jacket potatoes, with grated cheese — that's *au gratin* to you — and baked beans, and baked apple and custard for pud. Plain, simple homely food, fit for a king, or,' she giggled, 'a Pope.'

They both laughed in the way that only friends could at a mild joke, and then Poppy went upstairs to change. She heard Jacky come in while she was in the bathroom, and was glad that she would be there too when she tried to explain about Dr Fordyce and his strange attitude towards her. For the more she thought about it, the stronger grew her conviction that the doctor had some sort of grudge against her; his manner each time she had come into contact with him seemed to prove that. Perhaps if she discussed it with Ruth and Jacky, some reason, although this didn't seem likely, might emerge to explain his behaviour, and if she knew what was bugging him she could perhaps do something about it.

They talked about it over supper, and Jacky suggested, mostly in fun, that the doctor, newly arrived at Princes, and therefore still something of an unknown quantity, might see in Poppy similarities to a girlfriend who had just parted from him.

'He can't bear to look at you,' she said, looking soulful, 'because you remind him of the girl who has just broken his heart.'

'Rubbish,' said Ruth, and added humorously, 'The trouble with you, old thing, is that on account of Giles Wilding, registrar, presently practising in this hospital, to whom you are affianced, you see everything through rose-coloured romantic glasses. It's much more likely that our handsome Dr Fordyce had indigestion or something, and that's why he gave Poppy the cold shoulder.'

'What, indigestion several times? And then he only gave the cold shoulder to me, not any other staff, and certainly not to the kids, with whom he is great. You should see him with them; he's fantastic, and they love him. He's got these dark brown eyes that can slay you, but they wrinkle when he's talking to the children, and in spite of being. . .' She stopped, realising that both her friends were staring hard at her. 'What's the matter?' she asked. 'Why are you looking at me like that?'

'Oh, no,' they both said in unison. 'So that's the way the cookie crumbles.'

'What on earth do you mean? I don't understand.'

'Well, Poppy, really, can't you see what's happened?' asked Jacky. 'No wonder you think that he's acting strangely with you.'

'I don't know what you're talking about.'

'I don't think that she does,' said Ruth. 'Though it's as plain as it can be.'

'What?' Poppy almost shouted in exasperation. 'What's as plain as can be?'

'That you've fallen madly in love with the good doctor, or at least the old chemistry's been at work, and you feel drawn to him, like a bee to honey.'

Poppy stared at her two friends in amazement. 'What utter, sheer, stupid nonsense,' she said. 'I only met the man yesterday, and almost disliked him on sight when he gave me that beastly look.'

'But you didn't dislike him, that's the point, and you remembered all sorts of things about him — how he looked, the colour of his eyes, and so on. It bothered you that he didn't fall over himself to be nice to you. You probably imagined that look anyway, and his coolness today. It's you who have been seeing him all wrong, not the other way around, and it's because of how you feel about him that he seems to have been cool towards you. He's the nice guy that everyone thinks he is; it's you who's seeing him differently,' said Ruth.

'What is this,' said Poppy, 'a lecture on the anatomy of love? Dear God, please give me strength to put up with these idiots.'

Ruth and Jacky both laughed at her exasperated

remark. The rest of the evening passed off as usual, with the three of them watching the television, and intermittently discussing the details of Jacky's wedding arrangements. She was to be married in the spring, and Poppy and Ruth were to be bridesmaids.

Lying in bed later, Poppy tried to unravel the mystery of Nicholas Fordyce's peculiar attitude towards her. In spite of the gentle fun that her friends had made of her, she knew that he had behaved strangely; she hadn't imagined it, and she certainly wasn't in love with the man. True, she had taken in his appearance, had liked the look of his long, narrow face, and dark brown eyes and hair, but this didn't mean that she was in love with him, just observant. The very idea was a joke. For a moment she wondered if he had noticed her honey-blonde hair, and fringe, and hazel-green eyes. What nonsense. She gave a little snort of derision, and after a while snuggled down comfortably into her duvet, and went to sleep.

The following morning her car wouldn't start. It wasn't surprising, as it had stood outside all night, and the plastic cover hadn't apparently been proof against the bitter weather.

'It isn't just a de-icer that I need,' Poppy muttered as she tried to turn the engine, 'or a strange registrar to wield one, but a blasted rocket.'

She knew that there was no hope of getting the car going in time to get to work. She looked hopefully up at Ruth's bedroom window. Ruth was on late, but if she was awake now she might agree to doing a switch and let Poppy use her car, which had been in the garage all night, and drive Poppy's car to the hospital

later, but her curtains were still tightly drawn against
the winter day. No way could she consider waking her.
Jacky had a day off, but her car was going in for a
service, so she couldn't borrow that.

She would just have to catch a bus, which meant
that she was going to be late on duty. Buses going
right up to the hospital only ran every half-hour, but if
she got herself to the foot of the mile-long drive she
could probably hitch a lift from the gates. She would
get the first bus going that way.

Poppy joined the queue of people waiting for the
bus, stamping their feet and coughing and shivering in
the bitter cold as they grumbled about public
transport.

'Reckon it's late again this morning,' said the young
woman standing next to Poppy. 'Honestly, it has been
every morning this week; it makes you sick, doesn't
it?'

'Well, I'm lucky, I don't often have to catch the bus,
but my car wouldn't start this morning.'

'Iced-up, I suppose, like ours was. My husband uses
ours for work, but he goes in the opposite direction,
so he can't even give me a lift to the office. You're
lucky having a car of your own, I'm saving up for one,
but I just can't afford it yet, what with the mortgage
and everything.'

'Mine was a present from my father,' said Poppy,
somehow feeling that she had to explain her car away
to this young woman of about her own age, burdened
with a mortgage and the responsibilities of married
life.

'Lucky you; wish my dad could afford to give me a

car as a present,' she said, making Poppy feel even worse.

Shortly after this exchange the bus arrived, and the queue surged forward. There were a lot of people ahead of her, and the bus was already quite full. She just prayed that she would be able to get on; if she couldn't, she would simply have to start walking.

There was a toot of a horn from behind the bus, and a white Range Rover slowed to a halt on the double yellow lines. Poppy turned to look, thinking how silly it was to sound a horn at a bus that had to stop to pick up passengers, and saw that the driver of the vehicle was Dr Fordyce, and he was signalling impatiently for her to join him.

She would have loved to ignore him, and hop on the bus, but the chances of her getting aboard looked less likely the nearer she got, as it was filling up fast.

She ran the short distance to the Range Rover. The doctor had the passenger door open by the time she reached it. She climbed in, and rather breathlessly thanked him as she did so.

'That's all right, Staff; after all, we are both going the same way. It would have been unthinkable to leave you standing there waiting for the next bus; I don't think that you would have got on that one.'

'Yes, you're right, I don't think that I would have done.'

The bus was pulling away, and the doctor followed it. Poppy just glimpsed the last few people in the queue moving back on to the pavement, and avoided the eye of the young woman with whom she had been talking. It was on the tip of her tongue to ask Dr Fordyce if he would give her a lift too, but one glance at his stern profile prevented her. After all, she assuaged her conscience, the woman was a bit of a moaner, and there were other people in the queue just as deserving, and they couldn't all be offered a lift.

The doctor glanced sideways at her. 'Car wouldn't start?' he asked, but in such a tone that it was obvious that he knew the answer. His mouth twitched at the corners. 'Trouble with the lock again?'

Poppy shook her head. 'No, it was iced-up, right through to its poor little engine, even though it was covered by a tarpualin.' She giggled, partly because she found the doctor's nearness a bit unnerving, partly because she was genuinely amused by a thought that had just struck her. 'It's suffering from hypothermia, I think.'

'I'm not surprised, if it was standing out all night.' He actually grinned. 'Nice analogy—hypothermia. Haven't you got a garage?'

'Only for one car, and whoever gets home first bags that, and Ruth was off early yesterday, so the garage was all hers.'

'Another nurse?'

'Yes, three of us share a house.'

'Does it work?' To Poppy's surprise, he seemed genuinely interested.

'Oh, yes, it's super. You see, we were all in the same training set at Princes. We've been friends since school.'

'I didn't realise that you'd trained here; I thought a London hospital?' His voice ended in a question mark.

She shook her head; she was surprised that he'd thought of her at all, and seemed interested in where she had trained.

They turned into the drive leading up to the hospital. There was a figure plodding slowly up the drive ahead of them.

'I'll have to stop and offer a lift,' said the doctor.

He sounded put out, reluctant, Poppy thought, and then wondered if she had imagined it. I must, she decided, stop jumping to conclusions about this man. 'Of course you must,' she replied. 'I believe it's Sister Graham from Geriatrics, but she's so muffled-up that it's difficult to tell.'

Nicholas Fordyce grunted, and pulled up on the slippery drive, beside the figure, who they now realised, was limping.

She turned and gave them a wobbly smile. It was Sister Graham. 'Am I pleased to see you,' she said, as they drew up and Poppy opened the door. 'I slipped on an icy patch, and went down with a hell of a bang. I think that I may have busted a vein.'

Dr Fordyce, who had been sitting in the car with the engine running, ready to move off, switched off the engine, undid his seatbelt, and was out of the car in what seemed to be one fluid movement. He was at the sister's side in a flash, and bending to look at her leg.

'Which one?' he asked.

'Right. I can't really see how bad it is as I've got trousers on over my uniform, it being so bitterly cold.'

Unceremoniously the doctor pushed the dark trousers up over Sister Graham's shin. A steady stream of blood was trickling through the dark stocking that the sister was wearing.

'Yes, you have busted a vein,' the doctor said.

'You'd better go in the back, and Staff will hold a
pressure pad over it till we get to Casualty.' He pulled
a large white handkerchief from an inner breast
pocket, and handed it to Poppy. 'Fold it as small as
you can and apply direct digital pressure,' he said, 'as
soon as we've got Sister into the car.'

Between them they lifted Sister Graham, who was
quite tiny, on to the back seat of the car, and Poppy
climbed in beside her. As Nicholas re-started the
engine, Poppy applied pressure to the injured leg with
his folded handkerchief. It soon became soaked with
dark, venous blood oozing from the large vein crossing
the shin bone.

'You've damaged an anterial tibial vein, Sister,' said
Poppy, bringing as much pressure to bear on the
wound as she could.

'Oh, well, I dare say we can do something about it
before it gets out of hand,' said Sister Graham casually. 'Now, Staff, will you let Joy Cox, my staff nurse,
know that I'll be a bit delayed, but to carry on
regardless?'

'Yes, of course, Sister, I'll tell her.'

At that moment they arrived outside Casualty, and
Nick Fordyce turned round to speak to them.

'Stay put,' he said. 'I'll get someone out to see to
you, Sister Graham.'

'I could walk,' said Sister.

'No, you bloody can't,' said the doctor. 'I won't be
a minute.'

As good as his word, he was back in a very short
time with the casualty officer and a sister, and a very
grateful Sister Graham was transported on a trolley
into the A & E department.

'Well, that's that,' said Nicholas Fordyce. 'One
patient safely delivered into care. Now, my dear Staff
Nurse Pope, I had better get you to your unit before
Sister O'Brien goes hopping mad.'

'Really,' said Poppy, standing by the Range Rover,
'there's no need to drive me; I can easily walk through
the hospital from here.'

'Wouldn't dream of it, Staff. Jump in; we'll get there
in half the time, and I can explain to Sister O'Brien
why you're late, and take some of the sting out of her
Irish temper.'

'Dr Fordyce,' said Poppy, fuming, 'I'm quite capable
of explaining to Sister what occurred to make me
exceptionally late.' She gritted her teeth. 'Now, while
I am grateful to you for giving me a lift, I don't
need you to make excuses for me, do you understand
that?'

'Oh, perfectly Staff,' he said, grinning broadly. 'Now
do jump in, there's a good girl, and let's get on our
way.' He opened the passenger door of the Range
Rover and stood back to let her pass.

'Grr,' said Poppy, to her surprise finding herself
climbing into the vehicle. 'I don't believe this is
happening to me.' She looked hard at the registrar.
'I'm only going with you,' she said, 'because it's
quicker than traipsing through miles of corridors.'

'Of course,' said the doctor smoothly. 'That's why I
thought that you would rather drive with me.'

Poppy made some indeterminate noise in her throat,
and sat in stony silence, until they arrived outside the
Peter Pan unit.

She let herself out of the car. 'Thank you, Doctor,'
she said politely, 'for the lift, and for bringing me here,

but please don't bother yourself further; I'll explain to Sister O'Brien why I'm late.'

'As you wish,' said the doctor with a quirky grin, and drove away towards the car park.

CHAPTER THREE

BREAKFAST on Peter Pan was well under way when Poppy arrived on duty, full of apologies for being late.

'Well, I don't suppose you could help it, my dear,' said Sister O'Brien. 'Cars have a mind of their own, and if it wouldn't go it wouldn't go. Just make sure that it is in working order tomorrow, or leave home in good time to catch a bus.'

'Yes, Sister, will do, I promise.'

'Good girl.' Sister O'Brien gave her a beaming smile. 'Now I'll carry on with breakfasts as I've made a start; you take one of the juniors with you and make up beds for the admissions this morning. I've left the list on the desk in the office. There's one to be added to that; they phoned from Cas. a few minutes ago. A six-year-old had a fall and is slightly concussed—Trevor Hird; he's coming to us direct from X-Ray. You'd better do observations on him for a couple of hours, or until one of our medicine men takes a look at him, and decrees otherwise.'

Poppy collected the list, a first-year student, Lizzie Barnes, and a trolley full of clean linen, and went off to prepare the beds. She explained to Lizzie, having referred to Sister's notes, what each child who was coming in was suffering from. It was a very good way of teaching juniors and keeping their interest in the patients.

'This boy, Trevor, who is coming in from X-Ray,'

she explained, 'has had a mild concussion following a
fall. Now why do you think he is being X-rayed?'

'To make sure that he hasn't got a fractured skull, I
suppose, though surely if it was only a slight concussion
it's not very likely, is it, Staff?'

'No, not very, but it's a precaution that is generally
taken. Now he will be nursed flat for at least the first
few hours and we will do half-hourly obs on him
initially; you know — temperature, pulse, respirations
and blood-pressure, unless Dr Fordyce says
otherwise.'

They moved on to the next empty bed in the VIC
ward, and Poppy explained that a ten-year-old girl
who suffered from rheumatoid arthritis would be
admitted there later that morning.

'According to Sister's note, Lucy Brownlow has
been in Peter Pan before. She comes in for a reassess-
ment of her medication every so often. We'll put a
cradle in her bed to keep the bedclothes off her knees
as they are likely to be very tender.'

'It seems funny to think of a child having rheuma-
tism; it seems like an old person's disease,' said Lizzie,
adjusting the sheets and blankets over the frame that
Poppy had brought on the linen trolley. 'And I just
can't believe that it's all that painful.'

At that moment, the curtain at the foot of the bed
was whisked aside, and Dr Fordyce appeared, making
both nurses jump. 'You'd better believe it, Nurse,' he
said, rather sharply. 'Still's disease, as it is called in
children, or rheumatoid arthritis, as it is commonly
known, is one of the most painful conditions for
anybody, and particularly rotten for a child, who will
have to put up with it for the rest of his or her life. It

may go into remission at times, but there's no known cure for it at the present time.'

Lizzie went pink, and put a hand up to her mouth, and said, 'Oh,' rather shakily.

Poppy said, feeling that she must defend her junior, 'I don't think, Doctor, that Nurse meant that she didn't believe it literally, just that it's rather hard to believe.'

'Yes, I'm sure that's so, Nurse, but be careful what you say in the future. One can expect that sort of comment from lay people, but not from professionals, understood?' He softened his words by giving the girl a smile, which was the sort of thing, Poppy realised, that made him so popular with everyone. He was a tough boss where work was concerned, but there was no doubt that he was essentially a kind man, and generous with praise as well as blame.

Lizzie went a little pinker, and nodded. 'Oh, yes, Doctor, understood,' she mumbled, and returned his smile with a tremulous one of her own.

'Good.' He turned to Poppy, and the smile left his face. He said matter-of-factly, though politely enough, 'Staff, come with me, please. I'm going to examine Jonathan Copeland.'

'Certainly, Doctor.' She kept her face impassive, and turned to Lizzie. 'Nurse, you name and prepare charts for the empty beds, while I assist Dr Fordyce. Here's Sister's list to guide you.' She handed over the list and followed Dr Fordyce down the ward to where the four-year-old boy lay quietly staring into space.

The doctor stopped just before they reached the bed, and said softly, 'You have a rough idea of the history of this child, I presume?'

'Yes, Sister filled me in yesterday. Jonathan is withdrawn, and there is a possibility that he may have been abused. He is at present recovering from an appendicectomy, and his wound is slow to heal, which is why he is being kept in here, instead of being moved to the general ward.'

'Can you hazard a guess why I want you with me when I examine him? It's not an entirely medical reason.' He raised one well marked eyebrow in a quizzical fashion.

Poppy thought for a moment. There certainly wasn't any need for a nurse to accompany a doctor who was going to examine a child with a simple appendicectomy wound to be looked at, even if it was infected. It had to be something to do with the boy's emotional state.

'If the child has been abused by a man,' she suggested, 'he may be frightened of you attempting to examine him, even if he knows that you are a doctor.'

Dr Fordyce looked surprised. 'Very good, Staff, that's exactly the way my mind was working. But we mustn't forget that it might be a two-way thing with this little boy. No one is sure about the abuse aspect; he may simply be afraid of both his father and his mother. There may not be abuse of any kind; we just don't know.'

'If Jonathan is afraid of either parent, then he may be afraid of women as much as men. Presumably that means that we should always try to approach him in mixed pairs, doesn't it?'

'Precisely, though he seems to have accepted nurses in uniform without panicking, as far as we can tell. Let's hope that he starts trusting us all soon.' He looked at her very hard, his dark brown eyes boring into her, an almost puzzled look on his face. 'By the way,' he asked, 'have you done any psychiatric training? You sound as if you might know something about it.'

'No, I've never wanted to do anything but paediatrics; that's why I'm so thrilled to have got this relief job.'

She actually found herself smiling at him, briefly feeling in complete accord with him. He seemed for the moment to have lost his antagonism towards her, and be treating her simply as a colleague, and, what was more, one whose opinion he valued. Perhaps, after all, she had been mistaken about him. Maybe he was one of those people who needed time to get to know others, and that was why he had cold-shouldered her yesterday and on the day that they'd met. Maybe that was even why he was so in tune with the withdrawn Jonathan; he understood his reluctance to be relaxed with strangers. For all his air of authority, and his decisiveness where work was now, maybe he had been a reserved child, and could empathise with Jonathan. It didn't seem likely from what she knew of the mature man, but it was just possible.

His next words jerked her out of her reverie, and almost at once reversed her new ideas about him.

'Yes, well, I don't suppose it was too difficult for you to get the job, was it? I'm just glad that you seem to be capable of filling it competently.'

Poppy stared at the doctor; the implication he was making that she had somehow insinuated herself into the job astonished her. 'I don't know what you mean,' she said angrily, 'or what you are talking about. As far as I am concerned, I was simply next on the list for staffing on paediatrics. I'm grateful for being here, but I certainly didn't jump the queue, if there was one, and if that's what you are implying.'

'Oh, really,' he said in a flat voice, and she couldn't tell if he was surprised, but agreeing with her, or being sarcastic. 'Well, I think that we should be getting on, I haven't got all day,' he continued, as if it had been she who had been detaining him. He stalked towards Jonathan's bed, his shoulders stiff with what she assumed was dislike of her.

What the hell have I done to him to make him dislike me so much? Poppy wondered, not for the first time, as she followed him to the little boy's bed.

Once there, he dropped his aggressive stance, and was immediately the caring doctor whom she had already seen and admired in action with the children.

He sat down carefully on the side of the bed. 'Jonathan,' he said quietly, 'I'm Dr Nick, do you remember?'

There was no sign from the small boy in the bed; he continued to stare at the ceiling.

Nicholas Fordyce looked at Poppy, and she correctly interpreted the look, and spoke to the small patient.

'Jonathan, I'm Nurse Poppy. The doctor wants to have a look at your tummy and see if it is getting better, is that all right?'

The boy said nothing. He continued to stare at the ceiling, but his eyelids flickered a couple of times, and his mouth quivered.

Dr Fordyce bent a little nearer the child. 'I'm going to ask Nurse to pull down the bedclothes a bit so that I can see your tummy. It's not going to hurt. I don't think that we will have to take the plaster square off, not unless it's very messy. Does it feel messy?'

Jonathan very slightly shook his head.

'May I have a look?'

Jonathan gave an almost imperceptible nod.

The doctor stood up as Poppy drew the cubicle curtains round the bed and carefully turned down the bedclothes, and loosened the boy's pyjamas, exposing the small, flat abdomen.

The dressing was quite dry, but the area around it looked sore and swollen. Very gently Dr Fordyce pressed his long fingers over the affected area, watching the boy's face as he did so. Jonathan winced a couple of times.

'Jonathan, I think that I must have a peep under this dressing, even though it's not oozing. I just want to make sure that it's not gone yukky, OK?'

'OK,' muttered the child to their combined surprise, and his eyes slid down from their contemplation of the ceiling and focused on the doctor. 'What's yukky?' he asked, surprising them again.

Dr Fordyce looked at him for a moment, and then carefully took hold of the boy's small hands, and clapped them together. 'Yukky,' he said with a laugh, 'is sticky, and smelly, and uggy.'

Jonathan actually giggled like any other small child, and Poppy thought that she hadn't heard anything so lovely for a long time.

The boy wriggled in his bed, but let his hands remain in the doctor's clasp, and, knowing that he was being funny, asked, 'What's uggy?'

Nicholas laughed again, his long, narrow face full of humour and affection. He was obviously delighted with the child's response. He clapped the small hands together again, and said cheerfully, 'Now uggy is a trade secret.'

'What's a——?' began Jonathan, but Nicholas stopped him in the nicest possible way, by putting a finger over his mouth, and pulling a face.

'A secret,' he said, 'is a secret.' He turned to Poppy. 'Will you fetch a dressing trolley, please, Staff? And we'll get this young man sorted out.'

Poppy grinned at the doctor and the boy, and sped off, thrilled to bits at the way things had turned out, and full of admiration for Nicholas Fordyce, whose patience and humour had paid dividends.

The rest of the day flew past. Everyone was touched by the small, or perhaps not so small miracle that had occurred with Jonathan. It didn't of course alter the basic problem concerning him and possible abuse, but the fact that suddenly he was communicating made it more likely that he could be helped in the future.

Jonathan had obviously formed an attachment to Nicholas, his eyes following him whenever he was around. As it happened, the doctor was in and out of the ward several times during the day, checking on new admissions, and he never failed to make contact with the boy whenever he was near by.

Sister sent Poppy to assist the doctor when he was examining Lucy Brownlow, the ten-year-old girl with Still's disease. 'You know how much care must be taken, Staff, don't you, to move the poor child's limbs very gently? They are sore almost all the time. Don't try to rush; Doctor won't expect it. He's very under-standing about this sort of thing, and he asked especially that you should help him. Must have been on account of your success this morning with little Jonathan. Nicholas says that you have a gentle touch.'

Poppy felt herself blushing with a mixture of pride that the doctor had recognised her nursing skill, and irritation that he had singled her out when he seemed to dislike her so much. Always honest, she told Sister that she'd had very little to do with Jonathan's return to communicating.

'It was all down to Dr Fordyce, Sister,' she explained. 'I just stood around and did as I was told.'

'Well, whatever it was, it pleased our nice registrar, whose standards are sky-high where the kids are concerned. He seems to think well of you. Now run along and get an examination trolley ready; Nicholas will be here in about five minutes.'

It was a very simple trolley to lay up. Just the usual things like the sphygmomanometer, and various instruments for testing reactions, such as the patella hammer, which the doctor would almost certainly not use on Lucy with her painful joints, but which was obligatory on an examination trolley. Poppy added the ophthalmoscope for examination of eyes, and the auriscope for ears, spatulas, syringes for pain-relieving injections, and wipes, and receivers for used materials. On the bottom shelf she put some general dressing packs, bandages — straight and tubigrip — and light-weight splints, just in case the doctor decided to splint any limb, which could occasionally happen with rheumatoid arthritis cases.

She stood back and checked the trolley. It was ridiculous to feel nervous and wonder if she had left anything off; she'd laid up hundreds of similar trolleys during her nursing career, and had never had any qualms about it. So why now? she asked herself, I'm like a junior straight out of training school, laying up my first trolley. It's ridiculous; just because the man patronises you with a few words of praise, you're acting like a nervous schoolgirl.

'Pull yourself together, Pope,' she said out loud. 'Be your age.'

'And what age is that?' asked a voice from the doorway — Dr Fordyce's voice, deep, pleasant and drawling with humour, or sarcasm; it could be either, Poppy thought.

She kept her back to the door of the dressings room, and swallowed a couple of times, willing herself not to blush, not to give herself away to this arrogant man who was standing behind her. She must not let him see that he affected her in any way. When she turned to face him, her nice hazel-green eyes held their usual friendly expression beneath the golden-blonde fringe of hair. Her well marked lips smiled, and, to her relief, her voice came out sounding quite firm and cool, but holding a hint of amusement.

'Why, Doctor,' she said, adding a little trill of laughter for effect, 'you know no gentleman should ever ask a lady that.'

'Who said that I was a gentleman?' asked the doctor, an innocent gleam in his eye.

'I rather took it for granted that you were,' said Poppy, and added silkily, 'but perhaps that was a mistake.'

For just a few moments, his eyes caught and held hers, and nothing but fun registered in them — fun and friendliness. The hard or blank expression with which he had hitherto regarded her seemed to have vanished.

Was the miracle of Jonathan responsible for this softened approach? she wondered.

There was a brief silence as they surveyed each other, and then the doctor turned on his heel, saying over his shoulder, 'Well, I'm ready to look at this poor child when you are, Staff. Shall we make a start?' He moved smartly down the corridor.

Poppy sighed silently; evidently, she thought, nothing's changed. He still treats me like something nasty that the cat's brought in; he just forgot himself for the moment, and was accidentally nice to me. I just wish that I knew why he disliked me so much.

When Poppy reached Lucy's bedside, she found the girl and the doctor deep in conversation. Nicholas was sitting on a chair beside the bed, not on it on this occasion, Poppy noted, as he had been on Jonathan's. He obviously realised that the slightest jarring of the bed could be painful to the young patient, but, as with the boy, he was now working his magic on Lucy.

Lucy, for the first time since her admission, was laughing and relaxed.

'Hello, Nurse Poppy,' she said when Poppy appeared with the trolley. 'Dr Nick and I are just going through his badges.' She put out a small mis-shapen hand, with knobbly red joints, and touched one of the badges on Nicholas's white coat. 'There's Yogi Bear,' she said with a giggle. She touched another badge. 'And there's Jason Donovan and Kylie Minogue — aren't they brilliant? And here's Bart Simpson.' She jabbed a crooked forefinger at another painted face on one of the badges, and then quite suddenly subsided against her mountain of soft pillows, looking exhausted.

Nicholas stood up and bent over her and produced his gentle smile. 'Well, madam,' he said, 'taking a trip round my badges seems to have had the desired effect of subduing you a little.' Lucy managed a small smile. 'Now do you mind if I get on with my job, and examine all your lumps and bumps?'

He had struck the right note, not treating Lucy as a child, but as a sensible young adult, and one who needed special care and attention.

Poppy was astonished by the wave of admiration that washed over her. This was a doctor whom she could admire whole-heartedly, a doctor who began to meet the stringent requirements that she had laid down for herself, who in some way matched up to her father's disciplined lifestyle where his work was concerned. To compare anyone with her father where the care of children was concerned was an enormous compliment, and one that she seldom paid. Her ex-fiancé had almost qualified, but had betrayed her trust in him when his interest in her proved to be only a stepping-stone to her father's favours. His appalling treatment of her made him despicable, and she still bore the emotional scars, and was wary of getting too close to a man because of it.

Hastily she dragged her thoughts from the past to the present, and gave her full and undivided attention to assisting with Lucy's examination. Working slowly, so as not to distress the child with abrupt movements, the doctor examined Lucy carefully, paying particular attention to her eyes. Poppy, knowing that the cornea of the eye could sometimes be affected by the rheumatic condition, prayed that the little girl would be spared that additional problem, and for the moment at least it seemed that Lucy's eyes were fine.

'I'll just get one of my clever colleagues in the eye department to check them out while you're with us,' Nicholas explained to the child, 'but they're fine at the moment. But it is important to tell us if you notice any pain or cloudiness in your eyes. The sooner we know if anything is amiss, the more likely we are to be able to do something about it.'

'Don't worry, Dr Nick, I'll scream my head off if anything starts to go wrong. I don't know what I should do if I can't read and paint—well, at least as long as my hands will hold out.'

Poppy, used though she was to seeing people come to terms with all sorts of disabling conditions, had difficulty in controlling her emotions where this child was concerned. Lucy, once over the initial trauma of her admission, was so brave and matter-of-fact about herself.

Nicholas took Lucy's twisted and sore hands gently in his, and very carefully examined them, rubbing his thumbs over the enlarged wrist joints, and watching Lucy's face to test her reaction. She winced slightly, but didn't seem in too much pain from the slight pressure that the doctor put on them.

'Well I think you're good for a few more years of painting, Lucy,' he said, and asked with genuine interest, 'What do you paint?'

'Animals mostly, birds especially, because there are plenty in the garden, and flowers and things, but I'm into cartoons too; I usually do some for the school magazine.'

'I'd like to see your work some time, Lucy, if I may?'

'Course, I'll get my mum to bring in my folder, and you can see them too, Nurse Poppy. I've got lots there, and you can see the improvement that I've made over the years, as I've got older.' This was said with the unselfconsciousness of a child of ten for whom a year was a long time. A child, too, who had matured quickly in many ways, because of her disability.

Poppy and Nicholas exchanged smiles.

'We'll both look forward to seeing them,' said the doctor, and turned to Poppy. 'Won't we, Staff?'

'We certainly will.' Poppy smiled at him again, and he returned her smile, openly and frankly.

It had been a nice uncomplicated smile, Poppy thought later as she dismantled the trolley. Whatever the reason Nicholas Fordyce disliked her, it didn't extend to their work. In fact he seems to find me more than satisfactory, mused Poppy, disposing of a dismembered syringe into the sealed container, to ask for me to assist him with his examinations.

The more she saw of the doctor at work with the children, the more she admired him and the more she was reminded of her father. Thinking of her father made her decide to go home on her days off, which followed the party that her friends had dreamed up for Sunday to celebrate her move to paediatrics. She would go up to town on Monday, and return to Princes Park on Wednesday morning, in time for late duty.

Satisfied and pleased with her plans, for she loved seeing her father and hearing about his work, she busied herself giving the dressings room a general tidy around after she'd finished dealing with her own trolley.

She hummed happily to herself, anticipating both the party and her days off. The door to the room was wide open, and she heard footsteps approaching along the corridor. She knew that they belonged to Nicholas Fordyce; there was something about the long, easy strides, and the firm way that he put his feet down, that she recognised.

Had there been time, she would have got down from the stepped stool on which she was perched, and closed the door, but there wasn't time. She had to stay put, although the last thing she wanted at the moment was an encounter with the doctor that might spoil the friendly vibes that had existed between them over the afternoon. Perhaps, she thought optimistically, he won't see me in here. She pressed herself as close to the shelves as she could, and hardly dared to breathe.

The footsteps slowed down, and stopped. The doctor peered round the wide-open door, and Poppy felt an absolute fool, squashed up against the shelves.

'Ah, there you are,' he said. 'Sister thought that you would be tidying up in here.'

Poppy eased herself into a more comfortable position. 'Oh, does Sister want me?' she asked brightly.

'No, I do.'

'Why, is something wrong?' Her mind zoomed back over the afternoon's activities. 'I'm sorry, I thought that you'd finished with the new patients for today, but I can easily re-lay the trolley.'

'Nothing to do with patients. I understand from Sister that you are due off duty soon, so there wouldn't be much time for you to do anything, anyway. I've come on a purely personal mission.'

'Oh.' For the life of her she couldn't think of anything more brilliant to say.

'Well, don't look so startled; I was simply going to suggest that I give you a lift home. It's a beastly night. You obviously don't live too far away from where I do, judging by where you were waiting for the bus this morning, and it seemed a reasonable offer to make. Of course, if you've made other arrangements. . .' His voice trailed off.

'I was going to catch the hospital bus down to the gates, and pick up another bus from there.'

'And get soaked in the process? It's absolutely belting down, icy rain, and it doesn't look as if it's going to let up, but if that's what you want to do. . .'

Poppy pulled herself together. The thought of a warm, dry ride home, rather than a wet, miserable one, outweighed any reluctance to accept an offer from the doctor, even if he reverted to his usual cold self when he was with her off duty.

'Thank you,' she said, trying not to sound too haughty, or too eager.

A wry smile lit his face, as if he'd known exactly how she felt. 'A pleasure,' he said. 'Shall we say — ' he looked at his watch, pushing back the sleeve of his white coat, and Poppy thought, as she had when he had been examining the children, what nice hands he had, lean and sinewy ' — in half an hour in the front hall?'

'Yes, that's fine.'

'Right.' He lifted a hand in farewell, and moved off with long, measured strides down the corridor.

Poppy let out a long-held breath, and sat heavily down on the stool.

'Wow,' she said out loud. 'I hope that you know what you are doing, Pope; that man's lethal. He's all male, and then some. Perhaps a good soaking and the risk of pneumonia would be less dangerous. No wonder half the staff's crackers about him; he's certainly rather super.'

She felt foolish even thinking such thoughts, and was embarrassed at having said them out loud, but comforted herself with the thought that nobody else had heard her spouting such rubbish.

CHAPTER FOUR

POPPY arrived in the reception hall to find Nicholas Fordyce already there.

'We'll have to make a dash for it,' he said. 'It's absolutely pelting down.'

Outside the double doors they stood for a moment under the rigid canopy that extended along the front of the building to include the ambulance-unloading area. It was more hail than rain that was sheeting down in great icy lumps. Nicholas unfurled the large black umbrella that he was carrying, and opened it. He put an arm round Poppy's waist and turned towards the car park, and held the umbrella over both their heads.

'Come on, Poppy, let's run,' he shouted above the clatter of the hail hitting the roof.

Together, heads down beneath the shelter of the umbrella, they made a dash for his car. It was fortunately parked next to the consultants' parking area, and therefore fairly near the hospital buildings.

As they ran, Poppy was conscious of Nicholas's arm round her waist, and of the fact that he had called her Poppy. There was something comforting about the two things coming together, as if he was for the first time thinking of her in purely friendly terms, and had forgotten that he had something against her, or simply didn't like her when they weren't working together. It

made her wonder yet again if she had been imagining
his reaction to her, or if she had over-reacted to him.

They reached his car and he let go of her waist to
whip the key out of his pocket and open the passenger
door. Somehow, against the wind and hail, he kept the
umbrella over her until she had slid on to the seat,
when he quickly closed the door and hurried round to
the driver's side of the Range Rover.

He switched on the courtesy light as he closed his
door, and they both sat quietly for a moment as they
recovered their breath after their run through the
elements.

'Wow, what a difference from this morning,' said
Poppy, breathing hard. 'Who would have thought that
a frosty morning could have turned to this?'

'And you're not exactly dressed for a downpour, are
you,' he said 'in that short anorak?'

'It's warm,' replied Poppy defensively, 'and when I
left this morning I thought I was going to drive to
work, and even when I had to catch the bus this was
perfectly all right as it was cold but dry.' She hoped
that he wasn't going to spoil their brief harmony by
being hypercritical or sarcastic.

He stretched out a hand and patted hers. 'It's all
right, only teasing,' he said. He smiled, and she
breathed a sigh of relief. He definitely seemed prepared to be friendly.

They fastened their seatbelts, and he switched on
the engine and let in the clutch and they moved
smoothly over the icy surface, pausing just before they
entered the drive to let an ambulance turn into the
unloading area.

'Looks as if Casualty's going to be busy tonight,' he

said, pulling a face. 'I don't envy them; this is the sort of weather that brings in the motorway accidents by the dozen.'

'Yes, I did relief on A & E not long ago, when there was a big pile-up due to fog. It was horrific; I thought that we would never come to the end of the casualties.'

'I'd just started on Peter Pan, and we had several kids in who had been involved. And children are always the worst to deal with when it comes to accidents; they seem so absolutely vulnerable, don't they?' he said softly.

In the light of the lamps that lit the long drive, which intermittently lit up the car's interior, Poppy glanced sideways at the doctor. His long, handsome face looked quite drawn and sad. She had seen a similar look on her father's face at times, when he had been attending a very sick or badly injured child and couldn't find a solution to the problem.

Quite suddenly she wished that her father and Nicholas might meet; she had the feeling that they would like each other immensely. Almost as soon as the thought arose, she dismissed it. The chances of Nicholas Fordyce and her father meeting, through her, were remote. Nicholas was being pleasant enough to her at the moment, but they had got off to a bad start and she didn't think that they had anything in common outside their work.

Of course, her father and he might meet in the course of their work, at a conference. Her father often spoke at such conferences, and she was sure that Nicholas was dedicated enough to attend meetings of the kind that would keep him up to date with his work.

Her mind switched back to the afternoon, and she

remembered 'Dr Nick's' gentleness with the children he had been examining. She thought of the way he had made them laugh and how carefully he had examined them to prevent them being frightened or experiencing any more pain than was necessary. And he had done it without being patronising, or talking down to them. He was, like her father, a truly dedicated paediatrician.

'Have you always wanted to look after children?' she asked.

'Always,' he said simply, and turned his head for a moment to smile at her as they waited at the foot of the drive for a space in the traffic, before turning out on to the main road of Princes Hollow.

They joined the stream of traffic going through the small market town. Nicholas said, 'And what about you? Have you always wanted to do paediatric nursing?'

'Ever since I can remember. I always wanted to be a nurse, and I always wanted to be a children's nurse.'

'I suppose it's—— Damn.' He pulled up suddenly as a young woman made to dart across the road right in front of them, a shadowy figure in the street lighting, and the headlights of the car, and the heavy, sleeting rain.

Nicholas had pulled up in good time, and fortunately the car driver behind him also reacted swiftly, so avoiding a collision, but the woman, trying to regain the pavement, slipped and fell.

'I'll have to stop,' said Nicholas through tight lips, 'to see if the woman is all right.'

'It's OK, of course you've got to see that she's all right.'

Nicholas pulled into the kerb and waved to the vehicles behind him to proceed. The young woman was leaning against a shop window, looking pale.

She came forward as Nicholas pulled up, and tried to smile, wiping the rain off her face as she did so.

'I'm so sorry,' she said. 'I shouldn't have dashed into the road like that. I misjudged the distance; I thought that you were much further away, and I'm in such a hurry.'

'Better to arrive in one piece than not at all,' said Nicholas sternly.

'It's easy to say that,' said the woman with spirit. 'But I don't suppose you've got two kids at home, and no baby-sitter. They'll be on their own, you see, since they came home from school, and I'm so worried about them.'

'Are you all right?' asked Nicholas, interrupting quickly. 'Did you hurt yourself when you fell?'

'No, just laddered my tights and grazed my knee a bit, that's all. Look, it's kind of you to stop, but I must go; I must get home. A neighbour's keeping an eye on the children, but she's old, and not very well. I don't feel that they're safe with her. I'll go down to the traffic-lights and cross.'

'Where do you live?' Nicholas asked.

'Beckonsfield Way.'

'Is that far from here?'

'About a quarter of an hour.'

'Walking?'

'Yes.'

Nicholas turned to Poppy. 'Do you mind,' he said, 'if we give this lady a lift? It can only be about five minutes in the car.'

'Not at all.'

'Good.' Nicholas leaned back and unlocked the rear door. 'Hop in,' he said to the young woman. 'We'll give you a lift home, and stop you from taking any chances again tonight.'

The woman looked doubtful for a moment. 'Are you sure?' she asked. 'I don't want to take you out of your way.'

'Quite sure, please do get in.'

It took them literally five minutes to reach the woman's home, a neat little semi-detached house in the tree-lined road.

'I can't thank you enough,' she said as she got out of the car. 'May I offer you a cup of tea?'

'No, thank you, we'll be off now. Take care of that graze on your leg; bathe it with antiseptic. Goodnight.' Nicholas raised a hand and then moved smoothly off.

During the rest of the short journey, they discussed the problems that must face some parents, and particularly woman, who had to go out to work and rely on baby-sitters. They agreed that there should be more crèches at big firms, and more cheap facilities where children could be looked after while their parents were at work.

'It must be an awful headache for people like that woman,' said Nicholas. 'Imagine wondering every morning if your baby-sitter's going to be able to take your child. It adds a whole new dimension to the working day.' He peered out at the wet darkness. 'Do I turn left here?' he asked.

'That's right, and we're third on the left.'

Nicholas swept into the drive in front of the Victorian villa.

'Nice place,' he commented. 'I must say, Princes do look after their staff well, both in and out of the hospital.'

'Yes, they certainly do. Even when I was a first-year student and had to live in, I had my own room and shower. And each floor in the nurses' home had a kitchenette, where you could make tea and snacks. Some places I've heard of are still pretty grim on living-in accommodation.'

'Princes Park is certainly rather special in every way,' said Nicholas. 'I've come to realise that in the short while I've been here. You must be very proud of it, having trained here; one always has a soft spot for one's training hospital.'

'Oh, I am,' replied Poppy. 'I wouldn't have trained anywhere else; it's a great hospital.'

There was a strange look on Nicholas's face, which Poppy didn't see, as she was scrabbling in her shoulder-bag for the front door key. He looked as if he was about to say something, and then thought better of it.

Poppy produced her key, and turned to Nicholas. 'Will you come in for a cup of tea or coffee?' she asked.

Nicholas hesitated, and looked at his watch, and then made a decision.

'Well, a cup of coffee would be nice before I wend my way homewards,' he said. 'Save me getting one before I rush off out again.'

'You haven't got to go back to the hospital again, have you? You're not on call?'

'No, I'm meeting a friend for a meal later.'

'Oh, good, come on in, then, and sit down for a few minutes, while I make the coffee.'

Nicholas followed Poppy through to the warm kitchen, and took off his wet raincoat, before sitting down at the table.

'This is nice,' he said. 'A real old-fashioned kitchen big enough to sit in. I like it. Much better than my modern, poky little affair, which is serviceable rather than comfortable.'

'Oh, where's that, your flat?'

'South of the High Street, not far from the railway station, there's a newish block built on the site of what was once the Station Hotel. For some inexplicable reason it's called Eton House.'

'Oh, I know it. There was quite a row about the old hotel being pulled down some years ago. Various societies were interested in preserving it, though it was in fact quite an ugly old building, typical turn-of-the-century railway architecture, but it had all sorts of connections with Princes Park, and the famous people who used to stay there years ago before it was converted into a hospital.'

'You know, you really can't blame people for wanting to hang on to their local bits of history, can you, in a world that's changing as fast as ours is?'

Poppy put a mug of coffee and a plateful of biscuits down in front of him, and sat herself down opposite with her own mug of coffee. She was surprised and pleased that he seemed happy to sit and chat for a while, and that his sentiments so matched her own. It wouldn't have surprised her if he had refused the coffee, in order to get away from her as soon as possible. In fact it was surprising that he had offered her a lift home at all, when he had no need to do so. He had taken her to work by accident, but really his responsibility ended there. She could only suppose that old-fashioned chivalry had persuaded him to offer her a lift home in the evening, knowing how she was placed for transport, and realising that her situation was made worse by the foul weather.

Whatever his reasons, she was grateful to get home dry and warm. They continued to talk about Princes Park, and the surrounding countryside, and the two small towns of Princes Hollow and Princes New Town near by.

'Do you know,' said Poppy, 'that a lot of people, especially old people, natives of Princes Hollow, still often refer to it as "the Village", as it has only expanded to its present size over the last forty-odd years?'

'Since before you and I were born, Poppy,' Nicholas said with a grin over his tilted coffee-mug, 'which brings us back full circle to this afternoon.'

'Does it?' said Poppy, thoroughly mystified.

'When you were preparing the dressings trolley, and muttering about your age. Remember? I asked, and you refused to tell me.'

'Oh.' Poppy felt herself blushing. 'Well, what I said then still goes.'

'Even if I tell you that I'm thirty, nearly thirty-one? what would you say then?'

'That you were very young to hold the post of registrar in such a large and important department as paediatrics at Princes.'

Nicholas grinned, but seemed unabashed. 'I wasn't

fishing for compliments,' he said. 'I meant if I tell you my age, will you tell me yours?'

'It's not really a secret,' said Poppy with a laugh. 'I'm twenty-three.'

'So you qualified about two years ago.'

'Yes, and stayed on at Princes on relief while hoping that a job on Children's would come up, and now it has, and I'm thrilled to bits.'

'What happens when the staff nurse you are relieving comes back?'

'Well, at least I will have got some post-training experience on paediatrics, and can apply for some jobs that I'm not yet ready for, and — who knows? — Janice may decide not to come back too soon after she's had her baby, even though the crèche facilities at Princes are excellent. Anyway, I shall stay on as long as possible.'

'I'd have thought that you might do better at one of the London hospitals,' he said quietly, looking hard at her. 'St Kit's, for instance, with its huge paediatric department, or Ormond Street, devoted to kids.'

Poppy drew in a sharp breath. Did Nicholas Fordyce know about her father and St Christopher's? No, surely not; he would have come out with it openly.

She said as casually as she could, 'But I always wanted to work at Princes. I boarded at a school near here, and, as a sixth-former, did part of my Duke of Edinburgh award badge by helping the sick here at Princes.'

'Oh, so you've been affiliated to the hospital for a long time.' He sounded surprised.

'Since I was sixteen.'

'Did you have any difficulty getting in to do your

training? I understand that there's a lot of competition for nursing places here at Princes, and they are pretty choosy about whom they take.'

'That's true, but I had the necessary exam passes, so it wasn't really difficult for me.'

'And good references.'

'Yes, I had no problem there.'

'I wouldn't have supposed otherwise.'

Poppy wondered if it was her imagination, or had Nicholas Fordyce suddenly become hostile again, or at least cool, and if so, why? She didn't have time to make up her mind.

He looked at his watch. 'Good lord,' he said. 'I must away. Thanks for the coffee — much appreciated; I needed it. Don't get stuck tomorrow with the car. I may not be on hand to pick you up.'

'I'll remember that, and thank you again for coming to my rescue today.'

Poppy escorted him to the door after he had shrugged himself into his off white, military-looking raincoat. As he belted it around his waist, she realised how superbly fit and masculine he looked, with his narrow hips, and broad shoulders. Thin he might be, but muscular he was also in an understated sort of way. She was surprised to find that she liked what she saw, and a fluttering, hardly acknowledged desire to know the man better flooded over her, to be dismissed almost at once.

Nicholas gave her what she could only interpret as an enigmatic stare, as he said goodnight, and walked out into the still heavy rain as it slashed down on to his umbrella. He made his way to his car with long, confident, jaunty strides, as if he didn't give a damn for the weather. He lowered his umbrella, shook it, and refurled it in neat, smooth movements when he got to his car, before lifting his hand in farewell, and ducking his head as he got into the driving seat.

Poppy waved in return and watched him drive away, then went back into the warm comfort of the kitchen, with its old-fashioned, oil-fired stove that also heated the water and the radiators throughout the house.

She was glad that she didn't live in the soulless, though no doubt very efficient bachelor flat that Nicholas obviously inhabited.

It was surprising that he was living in a modern flat, as he was clearly attracted to buildings more historical, more gracious. Perhaps he had not had time to search for anything else since coming to Princes, and had then decided that he would make do until he had the time to look around for something more to his liking. Or perhaps, she thought, with a little stab of disappointment, he wasn't planning to stay at Princes for long. He was very ambitious; perhaps he was on the look-out for another, even more senior post. Maybe he was even contemplating a junior consultancy in the near future.

The idea took a firm hold in her mind as she pottered round tidying the kitchen and preparing an evening meal. Yes, that would account for him living in a modern service flat, rather than somewhere more to his taste. It was a convenient stopgap.

Perhaps it also accounted for the fact that the grapevine was silent about his lack of romantic attachments, except for a vague mention of Nina Caldwell. He hadn't the time or inclination for a serious relationship; he wanted to climb the professional ladder as fast as possible. Well, good luck to him. If that was what he wanted, he was a splendid doctor, and one day he would probably end up as distinguished in the paediatric field as her father. It was just as well that he wouldn't be around for too long, for, in spite of his strange reaction to her at times, she knew that, deep down inside her, she was attracted to the handsome Nicholas Fordyce.

She had enjoyed the pleasant half-hour she had just spent with him, happily discussing all sorts of topics, and could easily believe that she had imagined his dislike. It was just as well that there wouldn't be time to become involved with him. No way was she about to repeat the disaster of her experience with Jeremy Franks, another ambitious doctor.

Her busy thoughts took her through the preparations for a casserole, which she popped into a low oven. Neither Ruth nor Jacky were due home until after eight o'clock, so she decided to change out of uniform, and have a bath and wash her hair before they got back, and they could all sit and eat supper together.

She had just finished drying her hair when she heard someone ringing the front doorbell. She scrambled into old jeans and a sweater, and raced down the stairs.

The door was on the chain as it always was after dark, so it could only be opened a few inches. The porch light was on, and as she opened the door she saw, illuminated in the light, Nicholas Fordyce.

She must have looked surprised, for he said at once, 'Yes, it is me, again. Hope I'm not disturbing you, but

I'd like to use your phone if I may; my car's broken down.'

'C-certainly,' she stammered, and pushed the door to, to release the chain, before opening it wide. He shook the rain from his umbrella, just as he had an hour or so before, when he had left the house.

'I'll leave it here to drip.' He leaned the brolly against the porch wall. 'And then I should like to phone the garage and my dinner guest, please. My car's not far away; I was taking a short cut to Wilmot House, you know, another staff residence, where I'm picking up my friend. At least, having brought you home this afternoon, I knew where to come for help and succour.' He gave her a wicked smile. 'Oh, and I'd better organise a taxi. I don't think that my date would take kindly to public transport.'

'Please do; feel free. The phone's there.' Poppy pointed to the wall above the hall table, where a pay phone was fixed. 'If you haven't enough change, there should be some in the box, but ask if you need any; I'll be in the kitchen.'

'Many thanks.' Nicholas moved over to the telephone, looking sleek and handsome in a black long silky raincoat over evening dress.

Different from the way he had looked this afternoon, thought Poppy as she shut herself in the kitchen. Then he had appeared rather dashing in his white trench coat; now he looked distinguished and sophisticated, his thick brown hair brushed neatly back from his high forehead, not a strand out of place. Try as she might, she couldn't help wondering where he was headed for, for the evening, or who he was escorting. It was someone on the staff of Princes, since he was collecting her from Wilmot House, a large Edwardian property accommodating a dozen staff in bedsits, or small flats. Medical, nursing and other staff were resident there, so his date for the evening might be almost anybody.

After about ten minutes, there was a tap at the door.

'Come in,' called Poppy, who had been filling in time preparing potatoes to go with the casserole, and putting on a fresh pot of coffee to percolate.

Nicholas opened the door and sniffed. 'Smells delicious,' he said.

'Would you like a cup?' Poppy asked. 'It's just about ready.'

'Love one, thank you.' He indicated a chair at the table. 'May I?' he asked.

'Of course, do sit down,' Poppy replied, her voice, to her dismay and surprise, rather sharp. Whatever had happened to her usual calm? 'Did you get through all right?'

'Yes, thanks. The taxi should be here shortly, and I'll drop the key into the garage on my way to Wilmot House. They're going to pick up my car tonight and I should get it back later tomorrow.'

Poppy poured out a mug of coffee and set it down before him. 'Have you any idea what's gone wrong?' she asked.

'Starter motor, probably. The car stalled and wouldn't start up again. . . But who knows? Diagnosing diseases in cars seems as complicated as diagnosing them in people.'

'How are you going to get to work tomorrow?'

'Oh,' he said confidently, 'Nina will lend me her little Fiat. She's got a day off.'

Poppy turned back to the oven and busied herself with the boiling pot of potatoes. In an even voice, she said, 'Nina? Nina Caldwell?'

'Yes, that's right, I was on my way to pick her up for tonight's do. We're old friends.'

There was a ring at the doorbell.

'I'll get it,' said Poppy. 'It's probably your taxi; they don't have far to come.'

It was the taxi. Nicholas swallowed the last of his coffee, thanked her for her help, and disappeared into the wet night and his waiting transport, picking up his brolly from the porch as he went.

Poppy closed the door on him, and stood leaning against it for a moment.

'Nina Caldwell,' she muttered. 'An old friend. Well, lucky old Nina. So the casual mention of her was right.'

She heard a car draw up on the drive while she was still in the hall, and guessed that it was one of the girls. It was Ruth, followed a short time later by Jacky.

They were both hungry and ready to eat straight away, and while they ate Poppy gave them a run-down of the evening's events, and her two encounters with Nicholas Fordyce.

'He must fancy you,' said Jacky, 'to have offered you a lift home in the first place.'

Poppy sighed. 'Well, to be honest, I did begin to wonder, even though he was still a bit off with me at times, but it must have been just good manners that made him offer to run me home, as he's definitely got something on with Nina Caldwell.'

'Nina Caldwell!' exclaimed both Ruth and Jacky in unison.

'Yep, he was off to pick her up this evening when his car broke down.'

'Well, I'm damned,' said Ruth, sounding almost offended. 'I haven't heard anything about that. Are you sure, Poppy?'

'Positive; he said so.'

'Must be a first date, or the grapevine would have been buzzing.'

'No, it's not that; apparently they're old friends.'

'Well, they can't be all that close, or we would have heard rumours of a budding romance. I wonder when our Nina got her claws into him?' said Jacky.

'Perhaps she hasn't; perhaps they really are just old friends. I suppose it is possible,' said Ruth doubtfully.

'Oh, you two,' said Poppy. 'You're always conjuring up romances. A man and a woman can just be friends, you know, like for instance Dick and I; we're only friends.'

'Oh, that's different; you've known each other since you were kids. He's more like your brother than a boyfriend.'

'Yes,' said Poppy, 'that's true. I couldn't even begin to be romantic about him.' She giggled. 'I can't imagine anyone being romantic about Dick; he's so. . . so. . .'

'Young,' said Jacky.

'Yes, that's right, so terribly young, at least in his ways.'

'And immature,' said Ruth.

'Yes, and immature,' agreed Poppy.

'But fun, and useful as an escort when there's no one else around.'

'Yes, we know,' said Jacky, and, 'You know, perhaps that's how it is with our dashing Dr Fordyce; maybe he's just an escort for Nina. Perhaps there isn't anything more in it than that.'

'Yes,' said Poppy, 'perhaps.' And she found herself wishing fervently that it was true.

It was a wish that invaded her dreams that night, when both Nicholas Fordyce and Dick Kendall intermittently escorted her or Nina Caldwell to all sorts of unlikely venues, with one man dissolving into the other in the strange manner of dreams, and she and Nina changing places at times.

She woke in the morning with a hazy memory of her dreams, and a stuffy headache, which fortunately vanished as she showered and dressed.

Her overriding thought as she left the house was whether her car would start without trouble, and to her great relief it did.

CHAPTER FIVE

POPPY wondered as she drove to the hospital how Nicholas was getting on in Nina's Fiat. It seemed funny to think of him folding his long, lean body into that little car; he fitted his Range Rover much better. In fact, man and vehicle seemed well suited, both tough and reliable, but elegant, she thought fancifully. Though, of course, she reminded herself, even a Range Rover could go wrong, just as a doctor of Nicholas Fordyce's calibre might have occasional flaws. She must rid herself of this notion that the man was near perfect, just because she admired his technique with the children. After all, his manner hadn't been particularly pleasant towards her on occasions since they had met; she mustn't forget that he seemed to have something against her, for some unknown reason, and he could show dislike. The man was definitely not perfect.

Just as she was parking her car, Nicholas arrived in the Fiat, and pulled up beside her.

He got out and locked the car door and turned to greet her.

'Nice morning,' he said, 'if you like grey skies.' He waved his hand upwards. 'But at least there's no rain.'

'Or wind,' said Poppy, with a smile.

'Or frost,' he capped her remark, and returned her smile. 'Quite a welcome change from yesterday, all in all.'

'Yes. What's the news about your car?'

They walked side by side towards the hospital entrance, and his swinging hand grazed against hers. At his accidental touch she was engulfed in a wave of excitement that reddened her cheeks, and made her heart pound for a few moments. She caught her breath and moved a step away from him.

Nicholas gave her a sideways look, and she prayed that it wasn't because he had noticed her reaction to him. She coughed to cover her embarrassment.

'It is the starter motor,' he said. 'The garage hopes to fix it today, or offer me another car in exchange. Apparently they have to send somewhere for some spare parts, but at least by tonight I shall have a vehicle of some sort to use, and Nina can have her little tin box back.'

'Hey, that's not very fair; it was nice of her to lend you her car.'

'Of course, I realise that. How unkind of me to complain, looking a gift horse in the mouth, so to speak.' He gave a theatrical groan and pretended to limp. 'It's just that being doubled up in that toy motor car is so uncomfortable.'

An ambulance arrived very fast at Casualty a few yards away as they were about to enter Reception, and a doctor and nurse came out to meet it.

'It's one of yours, Nicholas,' called the doctor, 'a kid with an internal bleed. We'll probably want you down in Cas. later for an opinion.'

'Right, I might as well come straight away,' replied Nicholas. He turned to Poppy, and held out the coat that he was carrying over his arm. 'Be a love and put that in the duty office for me, please, and tell Sister that I'll be up a bit later to do my round, and warn her that we'll probably need another bed for this youngster, who will almost certainly have to be admitted for observation or surgery.'

'OK, will do.'

Poppy made her way through Reception to the Peter Pan unit, unconsciously hugging the doctor's car coat close to her body as she went, as if it were something precious. She realised this quite suddenly when she entered the duty room, and hastily slung the coat across the back of a chair as if she had been burnt.

'What on earth's the matter with you, Poppy Pope?' she muttered to herself in disgust, as she made her way to the staff cloakroom. 'What the hell is there about the man that makes you react the way you are? You dream about the man, he touches your hand and it feels like an electric shock, he gives you his old car coat to hold and you behave as if it were the crown jewels to be protected with your life. . . For heaven's sake, you're not a teenager; be your age.'

She realised as she said it that she had said the same thing before in connection with Dr Fordyce, and he had overheard her and teased her about it. Now she reminded herself, yet again, as she tidied her hair and pinned on her cap, that the doctor was not only just a man, but also a man who didn't seem to like her all that much at times, and who, in any case, was interested in another nurse. There was no point in letting chemistry or whatever it was get the better of her; Nicholas Fordyce, for better or worse, was out of her reach, and she might as well accept the situation.

This positive thought, once accepted, was comforting and gave her strength. She determined to adhere

to her own common-sense advice, and, feeling rather
calmer, she made her way to Sister's office to report
on duty, and pass on the message that the doctor had
given her.

She was busy from the moment she entered the
ward. Sister asked her to work in the baby cubicles,
and take a new junior with her to show her the ropes.
Since Poppy herself was only just getting into her
stride, this was quite a challenge, but one that, as a
staff nurse, she must accept. That was what staff nurses
and sisters were for, not only to use all their training
for their patients' benefit, she reminded herself, but to
help junior nurses acquire the same skills.

It helped that she had spent the last two years on
relief. She had learned how to pick up information as
she went, and her memory, always good, had been
honed to a fine point of receptiveness by being forced
to take on all sorts of new information at short notice.
Now this paid dividends as she instructed the new
student nurse, Faith Turner, about the routine pro-
cedures in the baby unit.

Together they visited all the cubicles, and Poppy
filled her in on the medical condition of each baby.
She helped Faith change and bath Baby Wakely, and
then showed her how to hold him as she fed him the
high-protein milk mixture devised by the pharmacy
department to the paediatrician's instructions. Baby
Wakely was suffering from malnutrition, she
explained, not through any medical reason, but
because his mother didn't understand how to feed him.
She hadn't enough milk of her own, and tried to feed
him unsuitable titbits of solid food to make up the
deficiency.

'This is the third time that this baby has been admitted to the unit,' Poppy explained to an astonished Faith, 'and for the same reason. His mother is given the food chart to follow, but either won't or can't understand it. Yet, according to the notes, she is a loving mother, and always returns to the unit when the baby begins to show signs of being undernourished.'

'I didn't think that things like this could happen nowadays,' said Faith.

'I know,' said Poppy gently, 'it doesn't seem possible, with all the help available, but those who need it most often seem the last to know about it. At least Mrs Wakely cares enough to get help.'

She left the cubicle, and went into the next one, where a little girl, Baby Henderson, was recovering from an operation on her bowel for intussusception. The baby was doing quite well, taking almost normal feeds, and in a short while would be fit enough to go home. Poppy attended to her small patient's needs, and then moved on, until all the babies in the cubicles were attended to.

When her work in the cubicles was finished Poppy went in search of Sister O'Brien to find out where she should work next.

'Do the medicine round, Staff,' Sister instructed, 'teaching the junior as you go, and then hold yourself ready to receive the admission from Casualty, the one you told me about earlier, an internal bleed. They're doing X-rays and various tests to find out what damage has been done. Apparently, according to the latest info that I have, this small child has possibly been battered.'

'Oh, no, Sister,' said Poppy in an anguished voice.

Baby battering was about the most distressing thing
that one could meet up with in hospital, and even quite
sophisticated surgeons had been known to give way to
their feelings where a battered child was concerned.

'I'm afraid so; Dr Fordyce rang from A & E a little
while ago about this child. The boy has an internal
bleed, the cause not yet identified; it's thought that it
might be through some external injury as there are
some bruises on his back. The police are involved
apparently.'

'How appalling, Sister. If this little boy comes to us,
where do you want him to go?'

'The first bed in the VIC ward next to the duty
station, to make it convenient for frequent obs. Move
the beds along to make room for him. I still want the
children in the same order, so simply bring the empty
bed down from the end, and shuffle everyone down a
place. Take another nurse with you to help you and
Nurse Turner.'

'Right, Sister, meds first and then the beds.'

It was quite a lengthy process moving all the children
down the ward. It meant moving lockers, and drips, as
well as beds. The children who were feeling bright
enough, in spite of being very ill, quite enjoyed the
experience, while the others simply dozed or remained
unaware as they were moved.

Poppy and her helpers had only just finished the
move and made up the new bed when Teddy Kent was
admitted from Casualty. He was a pale little three-
year-old boy with carroty-coloured hair, and huge
brown frightened eyes, looking very small and still,
lying on the stretcher.

Dr Fordyce followed the young patient into the ward, and examined him directly he was in bed, talking to him in a low, gentle voice as his hands carefully moved over his body.

Sister O'Brien had come from her office to see Teddy installed and say a few kind words. Nicholas spoke to her as soon as he had finished his examination, and nodded to Poppy, who had helped put the child to bed, to cover the boy up.

'I'd like Staff Nurse Pope to special this child, Sister, if that's possible. She's so very reassuring with these nervous children, and he needs someone with experience to do the obs. We think that the internal bleed has probably stopped, which is why he's not being transfused, though he's had some fluids intravenously. We may restart a glucose and saline drip later, if he can't go on to fluids by mouth, though that's what I'd like to happen by the end of the day. I'd like to get things back to normal for the boy as soon as possible.'

'Yes, of course you can have Staff to special. Do have a chat with her and tell her exactly what you want her to look out for. I've got to buzz off now to a meeting, so I'll leave the senior staff nurse in charge, and I'll tell her that Poppy will be busy in here, and I'll make sure that a senior takes over the obs when Staff Nurse Pope goes to lunch.'

'Thanks.' Nicholas walked over to Teddy's bed, where Poppy was already talking to the boy quietly and cheerfully, as she headed a chart to go at the foot of his bed, and checked up that everything that might be needed was on his locker.

She looked up and smiled at Nicholas as he approached, and he was suddenly aware of how very

attractive she was, with her slender figure, bright
hazel-green eyes, warm now with compassion, and
short honey-coloured hair with its little bouncy fringe,
looking very jaunty beneath her badge-speckled cap.
He blinked. It was almost as if he were seeing her for
the first time, for although they had worked together
and talked together yesterday he'd somehow not
realised how pretty—no, not pretty. . .lovely would
be a better description—she was.

He stared at her for a moment, but almost at once
his expression was one of cool professionalism.

Calmly he said, squashing personal feelings, 'Sister
has agreed that you should special Teddy, Staff, so
please start him on quarter-hourly obs for the next
hour. If there's no deterioration in that time, or signs
that the bleeding has recommenced, you may reduce
to half-hourly checks on temperature, pulse and respirations, but continue quarter-hourly with the blood-
pressure count. You may moisten his lips with water,
but he's not to have anything by mouth. I shall be in
from time to time, but, of course, if there is any
marked change in the boy's condition, you are to bleep
me immediately. Understood?'

'Understood,' she said. 'I think that I might read to
Teddy.' She smiled at the child. 'That should send him
to sleep.'

Nicholas looked momentarily surprised, and then
said rather stiffly, 'You've a very nice voice, Staff,
quiet and melodious; Teddy's a lucky boy.' He smiled
down at the boy, and gently patted his head. 'You be
a good boy, and do what Nurse Poppy tells you, old
chap, and you'll soon be feeling better.'

Teddy looked up at him with wide, still frightened eyes. 'Yes,' he whispered. 'I'll be good.'

Nicholas turned away, and muttered, half to himself, half to Poppy, 'I could have phrased that better. The kid's always trying to be good, apparently, to these uncaring, perhaps even cruel parents; at least, that's the impression that they've gained in Casualty.' He took a few steps across the ward, and paused at the door to raise his hand in Poppy's direction. 'See you,' he said softly, and vanished through the swing-doors.

The rest of the day passed quickly. Teddy began to improve, and by mid-afternoon was allowed sips of water to drink. Poppy instructed the staff nurse who was taking over from her to increase and repeat these small drinks during the course of the evening, as all the signs were that the internal bleeding had stopped.

She had been so busy during the afternoon that she had hardly noticed the outside world, and what the weather was doing, so it was a surprise to her to find that the grey skies of the morning had got thicker as darkness fell, and it had started to rain. There was no wind as there had been the previous day, and the rain was falling as sleet, and it had turned bitterly cold.

Her car was standing where she had left it in the car park, but Nina's little Fiat had gone, and standing in its place was Nicholas's Range Rover. Evidently during the day Nina had called to collect her car, and the garage had delivered the doctor's chunky vehicle.

Poppy smiled, remembering how uncomfortable he'd found the small car, and knew that he would be delighted to get his own back.

The smile faded from her lips as she got into her car

and prepared to drive away, and thoughts of Nicholas and Nina filled her mind. The thoughts hurt, which, she told herself, was ludicrous. She'd only known Nicholas Fordyce for a few days; he was ambitious and she didn't want anything to do with ambitious medical men. Once was enough.

The drive home was unpleasant, with rain and sleet being driven into the windscreen by the light wind that had sprung up since she started her journey. But she was distracted and cheered by the shops in the High Street, with their coloured lights and gaudily decorated windows, heralding Christmas. By the time she got home, her spirits had lifted, and when she opened the door to Victoria House, and caught a whiff of something very spicy and savoury cooking, she was her usual happy self.

'What are we having tonight?' she called.

It was Giles Wilding—Jacky's fiancé—who replied.

'One of my specials,' he shouted from the kitchen. He appeared in the hall doorway. 'Come on, Poppy, come and keep me company and have a glass of wine. Supper's on me tonight, and Jacky's upstairs making herself gorgeous, and Ruth's just come in and is hogging the bathroom.'

Poppy joined Giles in the kitchen, which was warm and steamy, and smelt heavenly, and Giles, she thought, looked rather like the kitchen, his fair, good-looking face all flushed with warmth from the stove, and his blue-striped apron greasy with finger marks.

Giles poured her out a glass of red wine.

'Sit,' he commanded, and Poppy, sketching a mock-curtsy, sat, and took a sip of wine. 'There's your post,'

Giles said, pushing a pile of envelopes towards her. 'All Christmas cards; I've checked.'

'Do you mind?' said Poppy, pretending indignation. 'My post is private and confidential.'

'Sorry, sorry,' said Giles with bowed head, and in his turn pretending to be conscience-stricken.

Poppy settled down with her drink to read her cards, feeling warm and cared for in the presence of this blond, friendly giant who adored Jacky, and for her sake loved her friends, and was also a splendid cook.

She had opened several cards before she noticed that the kitchen table was laid up with six places.

'Are we having visitors?' she asked Giles. 'Or can't I count any more?'

'Visitors,' said Giles. 'One of my colleagues, a lone bachelor — well, not exactly lone, as he has a girlfriend who's coming tonight. But he's newish to Princes, and it seemed a kind gesture, you know, Christmas being nigh, and all that, to invite him, and his friend, over for the evening.'

All at once, Poppy had an uncanny feeling that she knew who was coming to supper. Casually she asked, 'What's the name of this chum of yours? Do I know him?'

'Well, it was going to be a surprise,' said Giles, looking uncomfortable.

'One of Jacky's surprises?'

'Well, yes, actually.'

'You might as well come clean, Giles, and tell me who it is; I've got a good idea.'

'Nicholas Fordyce, your registrar,' said Giles, looking sheepish. 'I knew you'd worm it out of me, and Jacky swore me to secrecy.'

'She would,' said Poppy laconically. 'Trust Jacky. I suppose it was she who suggested that you should take pity on Nicholas, and invite him and his girlfriend for a meal. Honestly, Giles, I thought it was a bit odd that you should feel that sorry for a lonesome colleague, but for devious little Jacky that's a different proposition altogether.'

Giles tried to look hurt. 'Hey, I'm not without compassion, you know. There was poor old Fordyce looking glum, and there was I, looking forward to supper with three stunning girls, and I thought——'

'Primed by Jacky earlier. . .'

'I told her that you wouldn't buy it,' said Giles wryly. 'But it was true that Fordyce looked pretty grim and upset. There was this kid who'd been beaten up—but of course you must know about that. Well, I just mentioned it to Jacky when I saw her, and she came up with the idea of inviting the bloke and his friend, Nina Caldwell, along for supper. I don't know why it had to be kept a secret from you, but that's my Jacky.' He grinned in a rather foolish fashion, and Poppy envied him being so besotted by his fiancée that he would do almost anything that she asked.

'I wonder what scheme's afoot?' queried Poppy. 'She didn't give you a clue what she was up to, did she?'

'Not an inkling, just said that it would be a nice idea to get to know Nicholas, and renew your friendship with Nina.'

'Well, we weren't exactly bosom pals with Nina. Her set was a year ahead of ours, but we've all worked with her at times. She's quite a decent sort.'

'You know, Poppy, I don't see why you should read

anything into the fact that Jacky suggested that we ask Fordyce to supper. Why not accept that it was just a friendly gesture?'

'Yes, why not?' agreed Poppy. 'I'm going up to change.'

There was no point in prolonging the discussion with Giles. She just hoped that she would get through the evening without being too much affected by Nicholas's presence. It was quite obvious that Giles was in ignorance about the situation between herself and Nicholas, and his strange, on-off manner towards her. Jacky, bless her, must have some notion that getting them all together on a social occasion might solve that mystery. Though why she imagined that having Nicholas in the house should provide a solution, only the rather zany Jacky knew.

The supper party looked like being a success from the word go. The food, cooked by Giles, was delicious, and the conversation stimulating. They talked about everything under the sun, from politics to the art of diagnosis, and Third World poverty to the latest affair going on at Princes.

It was a typical coming-together of people of similar ages, and with similar interests and background knowledge. It was great fun. Poppy, who had had reservations about meeting Nicholas, especially with Nina, found herself relaxing after the first few minutes, and joining in the almost festive mood that seemed to have taken hold of them all.

They were all young enough to be looking forward to Christmas and the particular atmosphere peculiar to all hospitals at that time. A feeling that the rest of the world was out partying, or at home with their families, while the work of the hopsital continued as efficiently as usual, though with a surprising amount of the festive spirit, filled them with a kind of pride in being separate from the rest of humanity.

It was Nicholas who put their feelings into words, when he got up from the table and insisted on giving a vote of thanks to Giles, as the cook. After thanking Giles for the super supper, and saying banteringly that he was almost as good at orthopaedics as at cooking, he went on to say, 'I'm the new guy here at Princes, so I hope that you will forgive me for seeming to speak for the staff at this great hospital, where you four ladies trained——' he paused to raise his glass to Ruth, Jacky, Nina and Poppy, in turn '— and where Giles has been resident for some years. But perhaps an outsider can see more clearly what a splendid hospital it is, and what wonderful care it takes of both patients and staff. It is a truly family hospital, and one in which I am proud to work.' He looked down at the tablecloth for a moment, and then raised his head. 'Well, if that sounds fulsome, I'm sorry, but it's just the way I feel, and especially now at Christmas time, a season that is close to my heart, as I was born on December the sixth, St Nicholas's day.'

'That's the day after tomorrow,' said Poppy. 'Sunday's your birthday.'

'Yes,' said Nicholas. 'I'm thirty-one on Sunday, getting on for middle-aged. What a thought.'

They all laughed as he pretended to totter, and sketch an imaginary beard on his chin. His eyes caught Poppy's, and the merriment in them changed for a moment, to something quite different; almost a hint of sadness lay in their brown depths.

'Happy birthday Sunday,' Giles chanted, and the rest of them joined in.

'If only we'd known,' said Ruth. 'We could have made this a birthday party.'

'But we are having a party on Sunday—Poppy's party. Come to that,' said Jacky, 'and we'll make it a double celebration.' She got up and started to clear the dishes.

Giles and Ruth also stood up.

'Look,' said Giles to Poppy and the two visitors, 'you three go into the sitting-room, and relax. I'll bring in the pukka coffee—not the instant stuff—when it's ready. It's Jacky's and Ruth's turn to wash up.' He steered them out of the kitchen. 'You can sort out about Sunday,' he said as he pushed them into the hall.

'So you've got a birthday too on Sunday,' said Nicholas.

'No,' replied Poppy, leading the way through to the sitting-room. 'It's just a get-together to celebrate my getting the staffing job on Peter Pan, and an excuse for an early Christmas party.' She smiled at him and Nina. 'It would be nice if you would both come.' She tried to keep the eagerness out of her voice, as she realised how keen she was that Nicholas should attend the party.

'We'd love to, Nicholas, wouldn't we?' said Nina.

'Why not?' he drawled. 'It could be fun.' He sounded casual, not seeming to care one way or another, but there was a gleam in his dark brown eyes, and a hint of a smile round his mobile mouth, as he looked at Poppy.

He wants to come, she realised, and was thrilled.

'Oh, good,' she said, trying not to let him see how pleased she was. 'The more the merrier; there's quite a crowd coming.'

'We'll look forward to it,' said Nina, 'though I wish it were my celebration for going on to Paediatrics.' She smiled as she said it, to show that there was no ill feeling. 'I put in my request weeks ago when I knew that Janice Walters was pregnant, and would be taking maternity leave, but you pipped me to the post.'

'I didn't even know that she was pregnant,' exclaimed Poppy. 'I was just sent for to take over, and couldn't believe my luck.'

Nicholas, who had sat down, and was twirling his wine glass round between his long fingers, said silkily, 'It's not what you know, but who you know, that often dictates one's professional life.'

'Oh, you mean having the backing of dear old Sister O'Brien,' said Poppy with a laugh. 'She always promised that she would do her best to get me on her ward, as I was so keen when I was a student, and she kept her word.'

'Ah,' said Nicholas enigmatically and with a wry smile. 'So that's who it was who pulled the job for you. I rather thought that you might have friends in even higher places.'

Nina said, pulling a face, 'Take no notice of Nicholas, Poppy. He thinks that I should have got the job, because I'm a year ahead of you; he believes that you've got someone pulling strings for you.'

'Well, I haven't.' Poppy held out her hands in a

theatrical gesture, pointing them at Nicholas. 'Look,' she said, 'no strings.'

Although she joked, she was annoyed and puzzled by Nicholas's suggestion. She was almost sure that he was hinting at her father's position by his reference to people in high places, but couldn't think how he knew of the relationship. He had been working in Scotland recently; before that, she wasn't sure where, but certainly not at St Christopher's, or she would have known about it.

'I see,' he said in an expressionless voice. 'But it seemed reasonable to assume that you got the job because of your connections.'

'What connections?' asked Nina, looking puzzled. 'You keep hinting at something, Nicholas, but you haven't explained.'

Poppy and Nicholas looked hard at each other, and Poppy was certain from the guarded expression in his eyes that he did know about her father. But he had apparently kept the information to himself, and hadn't even told Nina.

Her mouth felt dry; it was the first time since she had started nursing that her connection with Sir Rowland had come up, and then it had only involved Matron and a handful of seniors. Ruth and Jacky had known about it since they were all at school together, and had kept quiet about it, until, with her permission, Jacky had told Giles.

In a way, Poppy thought, facing Nina and Nicholas, she shouldn't mind any more. She was having her crack at Children's nursing, and had achieved it without any help from her father. Secrecy was no longer necessary. It didn't matter who knew of her connection

with Sir Rowland; who would care? But the thought
that it might become common knowledge made her
uneasy. After all, the fact that Nicholas had been
suspicious of how she had got the job on Peter Pan
proved the point. She had been right to keep quiet
about her famous father. Hospital politics, she thought
with disgust. What a lot they had to answer for.

Nicholas frowned, and then said in a quiet, but
almost cold voice, 'Well, Poppy, I seem to have
misread the situation. Obviously you've kept your
connection secret too long for *you* to suddenly make
use of it now. It doesn't make sense.' He shrugged his
broad shoulders, and gave her a long, straight look,
and a lop-sided smile that might have been apologetic
or simply placatory; Poppy couldn't be sure which.
'Forgive me if I've been boorish about it.'

He sounded, if not sorry, at least regretful, thought
Poppy, although she didn't like the way that he empha-
sised 'you', as if someone else might be involved. She
made herself give a cool little nod, and equally coolly
said, 'Of course, let's forget it.'

'Good idea.' His brown eyes caught and held hers
for a moment, and she couldn't help feeling pleased
and relieved that they seemed to have got over the
misunderstanding.

Nina said in an exasperated voice, 'What secret? For
heaven's sake, will somebody tell me what this is all
about before I go crackers?'

'Poppy's father is Sir Rowland Pope, professor of
paediatrics,' explained Nicholas in a flat voice.

Nina stared at him, and then at Poppy, and then
started to giggle. 'And you thought,' she said to

Nicholas, 'that Poppy got the Peter Pan job because he's her father?'

''Fraid so. It wouldn't be the first time that such a thing has happened, unfortunately.' Poppy wondered if he'd ever been passed over for promotion when knowing the right person was more important than skill or dedication. It could explain why he was so suspicious about her.

'Well, if you knew Poppy better, you'd know that she couldn't do anything underhand.' She turned to look at Poppy. 'Though why on earth you haven't used your father to get the teeniest leg up the ladder beats me.'

'And be always accused of having got on because of him? No fear.'

Nina looked at her with a half-smile on her lips. 'You are daft, Pope,' she said. 'I would have jumped at the chance of a little parental help, I'm sure that I would.'

'I doubt it,' said Poppy. 'It might seem like a good thing to have that sort of backing, but it can be a millstone around your neck. You feel that nobody ever judges you on merit, just on your connections. It's not a nice feeling, I can assure you, and there are other drawbacks to having a famous father, especially in the medical profession.' She shrugged, and, though she wasn't aware of it, for the moment, her eyes looked bleak as she recalled the man — her father's registrar — with whom she had been in love. He had used her to advance his career, and then dropped her when she had served her purpose. That, as much as anything, had made her wary about disclosing her father's name. No way was she going to have anybody else using her.

Nina said in an understanding voice, 'Poppy, if you'd rather, I'll keep this to myself.'

Poppy said quietly, 'I'd appreciate that, thank you.'

'And naturally,' said Nicholas in an even voice, 'I will respect your wish to keep your secret.'

Poppy met his dark, brooding eyes, and was unable to look away for a moment. She couldn't guess what he was thinking.

'Thank you,' she whispered.

'My pleasure,' he murmured, his unfathomable eyes still on hers.

She was glad that he was prepared to keep silent about her situation, but not sure that he believed that she had got promotion without help, even if she was innocent in the matter.

There was a rattle of crockery, and Giles appeared, carrying a tray laden with aromatic coffee, biscuits and mugs.

'Ought to serve this delicious brew in delicate china cups,' he said. 'But the girls have threatened to go on strike if I produce much more washing-up, hence the mugs.'

'Good coffee tastes great in anything,' said Nicholas. 'Who cares about cups?'

Ruth and Jacky came through from the kitchen, and everything immediately returned to the party atmosphere, which continued till just before midnight.

When the three of them were alone, Poppy told the girls about Nicholas knowing who she was, and believing that she had got the Peter Pan job because of it.

'And now he knows the truth,' said Jacky with great satisfaction. 'I knew that if he came tonight it would clear up the mystery about why he was being so odd with you, Poppy.'

'Yes, I'm glad that it's all out in the open; and Nina was marvellous about it.'

'And Nicholas?' both her friends asked.

'He may understand,' said Poppy cautiously. 'But I'm still not sure that he believes that I've come this far without my father's influence.'

'You must be imagining it.'

'Probably. It's just a feeling that I've got.'

Much later, lying in bed, she found that she couldn't rid herself of the idea that Nicholas still didn't trust her. The look in his eyes when he had said goodnight had been unreadable, as if he was still guarding his thoughts where she was concerned.

Eventually she pushed the unpalatable thought away, and fell asleep.

CHAPTER SIX

WHEN Poppy reported for late duty on Saturday, it was to find that the senior staff nurse was off sick, and that she, Poppy, was to take over from Sister O'Brien as the senior on duty. Considering that she had been less than a week on the ward, this was quite a responsibility.

'But at least,' said Sister, after giving her the report, 'there are no take-ins today, unless there is an emergency, and several of the responsible mums will stay and help with the afternoon feeds, and I'm sure that visitors coming in later will stay and tuck up their children for the night. Sister on the special baby unit will come if you need her, and, though I'm off, I'll only be out for an hour or so, Christmas shopping. You can bleep me later if you're desperate; I'll be down at the lodge.'

'Oh, I'll try not to do that, Sister; you need your half-day.'

Sister grinned. 'It wouldn't be the first time that I've missed out on time off,' she said. 'It's par for the course. Anyway, away with you now, and sort out your staff for the afternoon.'

Poppy, once she got over the first surprise of knowing that the ward was her responsibility, rose to the challenge and enjoyed it. The afternoon flew by, as she attended to the children's needs, talked to relatives, and organised the staff. As Sister had suggested, many of the visiting mothers, and some of the fathers, offered to stay and help, not only with their own children, but generally in the ward and play-room. Two of the dads, in fact, practically took over play-room duties, so Poppy was able to leave a junior in charge there, while she and another nurse attended to the very ill children.

The mother of a small boy who was recovering from burns, and had only recently been admitted from the burns unit, where he had received acute treatment, asked to see a doctor about her son's condition.

'Right, Mrs Carter,' said Poppy adjusting the child's intravenous drip. 'Just give me a moment and I'll see if I can get hold of Dr Fordyce. He's in charge of Bobby's case.'

Her heart gave a lurch as she said Nicholas's name. She wondered what it would be like, seeing him after the revelations of the previous evening. Would what had happened make any difference to the way he responded to her? Probably not on duty. Both he and she were used to being controlled and professional when working.

'Oh, thank, you, Nurse, you are kind. I hate to bother you, especially on a Saturday, but I can only get in at weekends, and perhaps for a few minutes some evenings.'

'Don't you mind about it being a Saturday,' said Poppy, giving the nervous young mother a reassuring smile. 'Weekends make no difference to us here.'

Which wasn't quite true, she thought; hospitals, except for Casualty, and emergency theatres, did slow down a bit on Saturdays and Sundays. There weren't any formal doctors' rounds, and no routine operations.

The ward routines were slightly relaxed, and, even though there were almost open visiting hours these days, the weekends always attracted a few more visitors, which lent a sort of holdiay air to the place.

Thinking of holidays made her think of Christmas, and celebrations, and her party tomorrow night, which was also Nicholas's birthday. She had known him such a little while that it seemed ridiculous to think of giving him a present, and yet the thought of passing by his birthday without giving him a small gift seemed wrong. Only wrong, she realised, because of the special vibes that had passed between them, or which had affected her, and which had nothing to do with the length of time that they had known each other.

She reached the office and telephoned Central Control with the message that she needed Dr Fordyce on Peter Pan. He came on the line within seconds, and she explained about Mrs Carter wanting to speak to him about Bobby.

'I'll be there shortly,' said Nicholas. 'You were right to ring me, Staff. Mrs Carter must be most anxious about her son, now that he's been moved from the burns unit to us.'

His voice sounded as usual, with nothing in it to suggest that he was concerned about the revelations of the previous evening.

There was a lull after this. Poppy went round the various sections of the ward and confirmed that all was well, and returned to the office to begin filling in the report book and cards.

She had only just got started on the outline for the report when there was a tap at the door, and Nicholas entered. Poppy thought that he looked tired; there were lines about his mouth and eyes that she hadn't noticed the night before, and he had a bluish shadow about his chin, indicating that he needed a shave.

'My goodness,' she said spontaneously, 'you do look tired, as if you've been up since the crack of dawn.'

'That's because I have been,' he replied. 'My junior went off sick in acute abdominal distress at four this morning.'

'Bill Marks? He seemed fine yesterday.'

'Well, he wasn't in the early hours of this morning. The relief houseman called him in for an opinion on a baby in special care, and Bill collapsed a few minutes after he arrived on the unit. He was admitted to ICU for observation. It's not known yet what's wrong; might be an appendix, but no one's sure.'

'So you've been on call since four, you poor thing.' Poppy smiled at him in sympathy, relieved that any embarrassment that might have occurred between them had been negated by the news. 'Would you like tea or coffee before you see Mrs Carter?' she asked.

'Please, either, though I seem to have drunk gallons already, but what I would like more than anything is a moment to shave before I see this lady.' He ran a hand over his chin. 'I haven't done anything about this since some ungodly hour this morning.'

'Feel free to use Sister's cloakroom,' said Poppy, indicating the door to the little room that led from the office. 'Though I don't think that she has a shaver point in there,' she finished, with a laugh.

'It's OK, I've got my battery razor with me. I just need a few minutes' privacy; seeing me shave is not a pretty sight.' He gave her a lop-sided grin, and his eyes twinkled. Poppy's heart jolted. She pulled herself together. She mustn't let his charisma get to her; after all, she wasn't sure that he even trusted her completely.

He went into the cloakroom to shave. Poppy made tea, and put out a plateful of little iced biscuits that one of the mums had brought in as a parting gift from her small daughter. The mother had explained, when handing over the tin, that, because they were Tricia's favourites, her little girl had been sure that that was what the nice nurses and Dr Nick would like.

A few minutes later, Nicholas came out of the cloakroom.

'I'm ready for my tea,' he said, rubbing his hands together. 'I feel halfway human now that I've had a shave.' He sat down on the opposite side of the desk to Poppy, and stretched out a hand for a biscuit. 'Oh,' he said with a beaming smile, 'alphabet biccies, my favourite. What have I got? Ah, how very appropriate — S for Santa. That's almost next door to being N for Nicholas, don't you think?'

Poppy found herself smiling back, happy to see the tiredness and tension drain from him. If only he could be as relaxed as this more often. Frequently, when he was not with the children, she had caught him looking very serious and thoughtful. It was something, of course, that went with the job of caring for sick children, and once again she thought how he reminded her of her father, and his approach to his work. It was as if both men had a dual attitude to life, which almost split their personalities into two: one part for the children and the other for the rest of their life.

Her father, though, had been a wonderful husband, and had certainly found time to make her mother and his family happy. Last night at the supper party, Poppy had glimpsed something of the other man in Nicholas, when for much of the evening he had been relaxed and contented.

Nicholas sipped his tea, and reached for another biscuit. 'I've got an R for reindeer this time,' he said, 'very seasonal. Do you know, when I was a child, I always had a chocolate Father Christmas and a chocolate reindeer in my stocking, and I used to pretend that it was St Nicholas, my namesake, who was delivering the presents. You see, I had a Dutch grandmother, and she kept up the feast of St Nicholas every year, so my birthday was a combined festival, and with Christmas to follow it was a very special time of year, which, when I was very small, I thought was arranged just for my benefit.'

'You must have been a spoilt little boy.'

'I don't know about that, but I was a very happy little boy. Whis is, I suppose, why I get so uptight about some of the children we have to deal with.' He looked at her across the desk, his brown eyes almost black and unfathomable. 'I used to pray, when I was little, that all the children in the world would be as happy as I was, and, do you know, I believed at the time that they were?' His voice changed, and grew hard. He stood up, and stretched, and ran a hand through his thick brown hair. 'That was, of course, before I realised that children, along with the rest of humanity, suffer abominably, and when it comes down to it we can do so little.'

Poppy put out a hand and laid it on his arm. 'Not everyone; not all the children, all the time, suffer,' she said softly, trying to comfort him. More than ever she realised how like her father he was, with his compassion for children warring with the clinical man of science. Knowing that the best thing he could do this moment was something practical, she said, 'Will you see Mrs Carter now? She seems to have difficulty with visiting, and might have to go soon.'

Nicholas stared at her for a moment, as if he had just realised that she was there. 'Oh, yes, thanks, Staff,' he said distantly. 'If I might see her in here?'

'Certainly, Doctor,' said Poppy, equally formal. She removed the tea-tray, and took herself off to fetch Mrs Carter, saddened by the distance that seemed to have suddenly come between them.

Mrs Carter was with Nicholas for a long time. Poppy guessed that, as well as telling her all that he could about Bobby's condition and prognosis, he was comforting and reassuring her. As she couldn't do anything else while the doctor and the visitor were in the office, she made another quick round of Peter Pan, confirmed that all was well, and then told the senior student that she was just slipping out for a moment to take her official tea-break.

'Dr Fordyce is in the office,' she told the competent third-year student, 'should you need him, and, of course, Sister on the special baby unit is available in an emergency. I'll only be away about ten minutes, at the most.'

'I'll be OK, Staff, don't worry.'

Poppy hurried out of the unit, and made straight for the shop in Reception, run by friends of the hospital. She knew exactly what she wanted to get. Once in the shop, she looked along the shelves for the cardboard box depicting Father Christmas on a sledge pulled by two reindeer. She had seen it on display only a few days earlier, but it was no longer there.

'Can I help you, Staff Nurse?' asked one of the ladies behind the counter, whom Poppy recognised as the grandmother of one of her patients.

'There was a chocolate Father Christmas with a sledge and reindeers on this shelf the other day,' explained Poppy. 'I can't see it now. I suppose it must have been sold.'

'No, it's not sold, it's here,' said the sales lady, ducking beneath the counter. 'We changed the display this morning.'

'Oh, that's great. I'll take it.'

The lady who was serving her, looking benign, said, 'I suppose it's for one of the children on Peter Pan. I must say that you take jolly good care of them up there. My granddaughter isn't sure whether she wants to come home for Christmas, she's having such a good time.'

'We try to make it bearable for them,' said Poppy.

'Well, all I can say is that you make a good job of looking after them,' repeated the pleased grandmother, 'and especially that Dr Nick. The kids all love him.'

'Don't they just,' said Poppy as she paid for her purchase. She wondered what the grandmother would think if she knew that the chocolate Father Christmas and the reindeer-drawn sledge was a present for Dr Nick on his birthday the following day.

He was just leaving as she returned to the office.

'I've done my best to reassure Mrs Carter,' he told Poppy, as she put her purchase into a desk drawer. 'But she's a worried lady, as one would expect. I'd be glad if you'd speak to her again before she goes tonight. She needs all the support that we can give her. I don't think that her husband understands what she's going through; he seems to think that because Bobby's out of the acute burns unit he's home and dry. Mrs Carter is more perceptive, and realises that there's some way to go yet.'

'Right,' Poppy promised, 'I'll see what I can do. She's a nice lady, and a good mother.'

'Yes,' said Nicholas. He stood in the doorway as if he wanted to say something more, but then shrugged his shoulders and left. The office seemed empty without him.

Only after he'd gone did Poppy remember that she had been going to ask him how he knew that Sir Rowland was her father. He hadn't revealed that last night when he had told Nina who she was, and the puzzle had nagged at her ever since.

As far as she knew, he had never been on her father's firm at St Christopher's — and if she had met him it was inconceivable that she hadn't remembered him. Presumably he had discovered that she was Sir Rowland Pope's daughter from a colleague, at some point in his career. But where, and when? She made up her mind that she would ask her father, discreetly, when she visited him on Monday, if he knew anything about the charismatic Dr Fordyce.

Firmly she took herself in hand and resolved not to think about him any more, and soon became so busy with a combination of office and ward duties that she found it possible, with a supreme effort, to banish him from her mind.

Sunday was busy too, though she was only on duty

till two o'clock. Nicholas didn't come to the unit at all, and she heard that he was busy all the morning in the special baby unit.

Her spirits soared in anticipation of the party that evening as she drove home directly after going off duty. The weather was truly wintry, bitterly cold with a sleety rain again falling as it had the other evening, only this time the sleet was more like snow, and inclined to settle on the icy surfaces.

'I wonder,' Poppy murmured, with a little *frisson* of childish excitement, as she drew into the drive in front of the house and stepped out on to a wafer-thin covering of snow, 'if we'll have a white Christmas.'

The house was a hive of activity, with lovely cooking smells emanating from the kitchen, where Jacky and Giles were busy baking mince pies, sausage rolls, and apple and cheese turnovers, a Giles speciality. Ruth, who readily acknowledged that she was no cook, had been banished to the sitting-room to do the decorating. When Poppy arrived, she was perched on top of a ladder, fixing a bunch of balloons to one of the decorated cornices that still graced the high Victorian walls and ceilings. There were already silver balls and thick interwoven strands of paper chains, garish but cheerful, looped along the old-fashioned mantelpiece and windowsills. The room was beginning to take on a decidedly party air.

Ruth called to Poppy, when she saw her standing in the doorway, 'Be a love and fetch me another glass of wine and give me a hand with these balloons; I need some more blown up.'

'Right, will do. I'll get your wine and then go and

change, and be with you in a few minutes, unless Jacky and Giles want a hand in the kitchen.'

'Oh, I'm sure they won't. Leave the two love-birds to play happy domesticity; it's what they're best at, yuck.' She grinned down happily at Poppy. 'As for me, I like being footloose and fancy-free, and I hope that there are going to be plenty of loose males around tonight, and there certainly should be among the vast crowd who are coming, praise be.'

Footloose and fancy-free males, thought Poppy, as she changed into old jeans and a floppy sweater. Well, there might be plenty of those around, but she could think of only one whom she fancied.

'And he's not free,' she told herself fiercely, 'even if he showed the least bit of interest in you, apart from having ferreted out who Daddy is. He is firmly hitched to Nina, and you'd better remember that.'

She gave herself a mental shake, wrapped up the little package of the Father Christmas with his reindeer, and went downstairs to join her friends and get into the party spirit.

A couple of glasses of wine and dozens of balloons later, and with seasonal music belting out merrily from the system, she was her usual happy self. The slightly sombre mood that had washed over her had gone.

Jacky and Giles had made a cake and iced it with the legend, 'Congrats, Poppy, you made it to peds' and, crowded underneath, 'Happy birthday, Nick'.

'We hope you don't mind sharing your cake with Nicholas,' said Jacky, 'but it seemed mean not to mention his birthday.'

Poppy felt her cheeks glowing, and hoped that it would be put down to the warmth and the effort of blowing up balloons. She would have liked to have said that there was no one she would rather share her cake with, but of course didn't.

'I don't mind in the least,' she said cheerfully in a throw-away fashion. 'I'm feeling very generous today. Why, I even bought my registrar a little present, to show that there's no ill feeling about him having discovered my guilty secret.'

She had been wondering how she could explain buying a present for Nicholas on such short acquaint-ance, and now she had one, and it had come out remarkably naturally. Ruth, Jacky and Giles teased her a bit about making up to her boss, but thought that it was a good idea, and wanted to know what the present was.

'Oh, it's just a silly little thing, a fun thing,' said Poppy. 'After all, I don't know him well enough to give him a proper present. I'll go and fetch it and put it with the cake; it can be a jokey thing from all of us.'

She fetched the prettily wrapped package down from her room.

'But what is it?' wailed Jacky, who was terribly curious, and hated a mystery until she'd solved it.

Knowing her friend's insatiable curiosity, Poppy, who would have liked to keep the secret until the parcel was opened, told them, explaining that she thought it appropriate for a Nicholas, with a birthday on St Nicholas day. She did not, of course, tell them of the small confidence that Dr Fordyce had imparted about having a chocolate Santa Claus in his stocking at Christmas time.

'Well, it's quite an amusing little memento,' said Ruth. 'How clever of you to think of it.'

Poppy, hugging Nicholas's secret to herself, smiled and said nothing.

'I suppose you haven't had a chance to ask Nicholas how he comes to know about Sir Rowland?' asked Giles.

'No, I was too busy yesterday, and he hasn't been in the unit today. He's been totally occupied with the Special Babies; they've several really poorly ones in at the moment, and, with Bill Marks off, Nicholas has even more of a load. By the way, do you know how Bill is, Giles?'

'Well, the good news is that he's not blown up a nasty appendix; the bad news is that no one can decide what's wrong with the poor bloke — whether it's a simple tummy bug, or something more sinister. He's having all the appropriate tests, especially as he only came back from a stint in Africa recently, and his condition may be due to something he picked up there. Just to be on the safe side, he's being kept in a side-ward, and it's no visitors at present.'

'Poor Bill, let's write him a get-well message,' suggested Ruth. 'Everyone can sign it who's here tonight, and we'll pop it inside a card tomorrow; that'll cheer him up.'

The party was an immediate success. Of course, the fact that everyone knew each other and was in the same line of business ensured that it could hardly be anything else. Poppy, dressed in a shot silk, billowy-skirted mini-dress of a red to match her name, stood just inside the front door of the wide hall, and welcomed everyone for the first half-hour or so. Ruth took top coats and anoraks and whisked them to one of the bedrooms upstairs. Jacky and Giles poured drinks and offered food for the first few guests, then it was a case of help yourself, and the person nearest the door answered it, while everybody mingled.

By ten o'clock, though it wasn't late for a hospital party, when people came off duty at all sorts of unsociable hours, Poppy had begun to think that Nicholas and Nina were not coming, and her spirits plummeted. It surprised her to discover just how much she wanted Nicholas to be there. Somewhere in the deep recesses of her mind she felt that this would mean that he had accepted her as a nurse in her own right, and not just a superficial success on account of her father. The fact that he had already indicated this when on duty, and had asked for her to special patients, didn't satisfy her. She wanted his complete and personal confirmation of her ability. For some reason, this was important to her.

It was ten-thirty when he arrived, with a gorgeous-looking Nina in tow. Nicholas looked gorgeous too, thought Poppy, waving nonchalantly to him across the room as she danced with Dick Kendall. Her heart bumped erratically at the sight of Nicholas, cool and sophisticated in a wine-dark velvet jacket, over a mulberry and white striped shirt, open at the neck.

She moved away from Dick, as much as floor space would allow.

'I'd better go and welcome my boss,' she whispered, 'keep on the right side of him.'

'You might introduce me to the gorgeous creature who's with him.'

'It's Nina Caldwell, you idiot; you must know her.'

'Nope, I would have remembered.'

'Well, it's true that she was away for a bit, doing private nursing, but she trained here, and has come back on relief, as I am.'

'I don't know her, but I'd like to,' said Dick firmly.

'Then come with me, and be introduced,' replied Poppy, puzzled that Dick didn't know Nina, for, even accepting that Princes was a large hospital, most people knew each other at least by sight. True, Nina really did look stunning these days, especially out of uniform, and the change from being a rather mousy, studious individual seemed to have come about while she was nursing away from Princes. It was just possible that Dick, in the few years that he had been here, thought Poppy, as she led the way across the crowded room, might have missed her, or not recognised her. He had an eye for pretty women, but might well have overlooked a plain one.

'Nina, Nicholas, so glad that you've come,' said Poppy in her best hostess fashion. 'Here, let me take your coats.' Nicholas handed her his short suede car coat, which he had already removed. There was a dusting of white on the shoulders. 'It's still snowing,' said Poppy delightedly. 'I thought it would have stopped by now.'

'It's very light, but nice and Christmassy,' said Nicholas, 'as long as it doesn't produce too many accidents.' His eyes met Poppy's briefly, and then flickered over her dress, and she saw admiration in them. He turned to Nina, and helped her off with her long, elegant blouson jacket.

Dick moved round from behind Poppy. 'Hi,' he said to Nicholas. 'Nice to see you socialising for a change; we've only met so far when we've both been hard at it, and our paths haven't crossed that often.' He turned to Nina, and switched on the boyish charm for which he was famous. 'And our paths have never crossed, or I would have remembered,' he said in a half-serious, half-joking fashion.

Nina went pink, and gave him a charming smile. 'Oh, but we have,' she said. 'You had just come to Princes and I had just qualified. That was three years ago, and I was doing my first relief job on the burns unit.' She held out her hand, and Dick took it in both of his, as if it were something precious. 'It's Dick Kendall, isn't it?'

'Yes. Look, are you sure we met three years ago?' he asked. 'I can't believe that we did.'

'It was only for a short while,' said Nina, in a reassuring voice. She laughed. 'I forgive you for not remembering; there were a lot of fresh people for you to meet. I was only one of dozens, and I look different in uniform, and I've grown up a bit since then.'

Dick shook his head wonderingly, and, to Poppy's surprise, swallowed nervously. She had never seen him like this before, not even when, a year or so earlier, he had professed himself seriously interested in her, and quite upset because she wouldn't respond to him. He was infamous for being lightweight, boyish and flirty, and never at a loss for a complimentary word, yet here he was, looking and sounding deadly serious.

Poppy glanced at Nicholas to see how he was reacting to this blatant display of admiration, but his expression gave nothing away. One eyebrow was raised, as if perhaps in amusement, but his eyes remained dark and unfathomable. He became aware

that Poppy was looking at him, and flashed her a
sardonic smile.

'Shall we leave them to reminisce,' he said, 'and
circulate?'

Poppy felt herself blushing, and was furious. 'Of
course,' she said, 'and you must want a drink and
something to eat if you've only just come off duty.'
She realised that she was still nursing their two coats.
'I'll just get rid of these,' she said, and, pointing
towards the kitchen, added, 'The booze and the buffet
are laid up in there. Please help yourself; I'll be with
you in a moment.'

She rushed up the stairs to the small spare room that
they were using as a cloakroom, and deposited the two
coats. She went into the kitchen and found Nicholas
there with several other people. Of Nina and Dick,
there was no sign.

Nicholas was ladling out the rich, amber-coloured
liquid that Giles had labelled: 'Rum Punch, potent,
not for drivers.'

'I believe that's quite strong,' she braved herself to
say to Nicholas, 'not to be drunk if one is driving.
There's another bowl here for drivers.'

'Yes, I can read, thank you,' said Nicholas, an edge
of sarcasm in his voice. 'Very sensible, but I wouldn't
take stupid risks. I'm not driving; there are such things
as taxis, you know.' He bent his head near to Poppy's.
'Does that make you happy?' he asked softly.

'Perfectly,' she said.

'Good.' He bit into a sausage roll. 'Delicious,' he
said. 'Did you make these?'

'No, Jacky and Giles did.'

'Do you cook?'

'Well, yes, I do, I enjoy cooking.'

'You don't feel chained to the kitchen sink when you do?'

'No, why should I? Nursing is my profession; cooking is a hobby.'

'A nice distinction. But do you ever hanker after domesticity rather than the professional scene?'

'I can't say that I do; nursing is the most important thing in my life.'

Nicholas looked down at her, a glass hovering at his lips. There was a strange look in his dark brown eyes.

'Do you mean,' he said, 'that you would give up a home and children for the sterile world of nursing?'

'I've never thought of nursing as sterile,' she said. She felt her temper rising. How dared this man whom she scarcely knew examine her motives for nursing? 'Nursing, especially nursing sick children, is about the best thing that any woman can do.'

'She can marry and have children of her own,' he said. 'That's the greatest gift that any woman can give to the world.'

Poppy felt her self-control snap. She had done her best to make up for Nina's defection with Dick Kendall, if that was what was making Nicholas Fordyce so scratchy, and there was nothing else she could do. Because he had some competition for Nina's favours, he didn't have to take it out on her.

'Shall we go through to the other room?' she asked coldly, half turning away from him.

'If you'll dance with me,' he said, touching her shoulder. He smiled. His smile, as she turned back and looked up at him, lit up the room and melted her temper. It seemed just for her. Perhaps after all he wasn't too bothered about Nina deserting him for Dick for the evening.

Poppy just had to smile in return. 'There's not much room for dancing,' she said. 'But I'll do my best.'

'That's all I ask,' he said, in his deep voice.

They went into the sitting-room and joined the couples clinging to each other, and circling round the space that had been cleared in the large sitting-room. Very aware of his closeness, of his arms about her, Poppy gave herself up to enjoying the experience. After all, if he was happy to dance with her, rather than prise Nina away from Dick, who was she to complain?

The smoochy music finished suddenly, and Giles's voice rang out.

'We're here to celebrate Poppy's elevation to Paediatrics,' he said, 'which she has long aspired to.' There was a round of applause. 'But,' continued Giles, 'we also have another celebration: it is Nicholas Fordyce's birthday. So let's have a round of applause for Paediatrics' new registrar.' There was a great clapping of hands and a few ribald remarks about growing old, and thirty-one being almost over the hill, which Nicholas took with smiling ease. Somebody started to sing 'Happy Birthday', and, while most of party joined in, Ruth slipped out to the kitchen to fetch the cake, which had been tucked away in the larder. She lit the circle of candles, and placed Poppy's little parcel on the tray beside the cake, before carrying it through to the sitting-room.

There was more loud applause as she entered, and both Poppy and Nicholas were urged to blow the candles out. Together they bent over the cake, which Ruth had placed on a low side-table.

'On the count of three,' murmured Nicholas, his eyes glinting in the candlelight as they met Poppy's.

Poppy caught her breath as her eyes met his, and then she nodded.

'One, two, three,' said Nicholas, and together they blew out the candles.

Everyone cheered, and Jacky stepped forward with a knife, ready to cut the cake.

'Here,' she said, handing a plate with two slices on it to Poppy. 'For you and the birthday boy.' She picked up the gift-wrapped package. 'And don't forget this,' she said with a mischievous grin, as she handed it to Nicholas. 'A little something chosen by Poppy.'

Poppy gave Jacky a furious look. 'For heaven's sake,' she said, 'it's nothing much, just a memento from all of us.

'I want to look at it in peace,' said Nicholas, and he took her arm and guided her out of the crowded room, past various couples, including Nina and Dick, who were standing with arms linked together. They were apparently oblivious of everyone but each other.

Had Nicholas seen them? Poppy wondered, and stole a look at his face, but it seemed unchanged, with his lips quirking at the corners in a half-smile, and a warm expression in his eyes. Surely he couldn't have failed to notice Nina. Could his seeming indifference mean that he didn't care if Dick was interested in Nina? No, it couldn't be that; more likely he was just able to conceal his true feelings, and carry on as if nothing had happened. Or, just as likely, he was so sure of himself that seeing Nina flirting with somebody else failed to move him. He knew that she would return to him at a snap of his fingers.

The kitchen was a haven of quiet after the crowded, noisy sitting-room. Nicholas pushed Poppy gently down on to a kitchen chair, and perched himself on the edge of the table.

'I want to see what you have chosen for me,' he said in a soft voice.

Poppy almost panicked, wondering what he might be expecting. She repeated what she had said before. 'It's just a little thing, silly really, nothing important.'

Nicholas smiled at her, and against her will, and all her efforts at self-control, her heart turned over at his smile. Inwardly she asked herself what was happening, and made up her mind not to let him see how he was affecting her.

Carefully he stripped the pretty paper from the parcel, and came to the cardboard carton, with its bright picture depicting Father Christmas, his reindeer sledge piled high with toys, riding across a forest of chimney-pots. Printed along the base of the picture, was a message — 'Santa Claus delivers his Christmas goodies' — but 'Claus' had been crossed out, and 'Nicholas' had been written in its place.

Nicholas stared at it for a moment in silence, and then glanced down at Poppy, a small smile tugging at his lips. 'You remembered,' he said quietly, 'about St Nicholas.'

Poppy nodded, her mouth dry, her heart thumping, her hazel-green eyes locking on to his brown ones as he leaned down from the table and bent closer to her. He's going to kiss me, she thought, and felt breathless. Nicholas stopped a few inches from her face, and then blinked his eyes, while his lips, full and inviting, hovered for a moment near her own, and then brushed across her cheek.

He pulled away from her and straightened up, and drew the little chocolate model from the box, studying it carefully. He chuckled.

'It's got to be the most thoughtful present that anyone's given me for years,' he said, and his voice was quite husky. 'It's too good to eat. I shall keep it to admire.' He looked down at Poppy, smiling gently. 'I shall treasure it.'

Poppy made a supreme effort to pull herself together. This was getting over-emotional; she was being swamped by feelings that were almost too much to handle. The way she had hoped that he would kiss her was ridiculous; it was as if she were a teenager all over again, and falling in and out of love at the drop of a hat. It was embarrassing, feeling like this about a man who only half liked her, only half seemed to trust her, and was involved with somebody else.

She gave what she hoped was a nonchalant laugh, and said briskly, 'Well, it won't keep; it'll melt, or go off, or something. You might just as well gobble it up right now.' She stood up. 'We ought to be getting back to the others,' she said, and moved towards the door.

Nicholas slid from his perch on the table, and reached her in two long strides. He put a detaining hand on her arm; his eyes, when she turned to look at him, were deep, fathomless, almost black.

'I haven't thanked you properly yet,' he said, and he drew her, unresisting, into his arms. He lowered his head, and his mouth came down on hers in a long, soft, lingering kiss.

There were voices in the hall, and footsteps coming towards the kitchen.

With a sigh, Nicholas put her gently from him. 'Thank you for my present,' he said, 'and for a lovely birthday party.'

And it had been a lovely party, reflected Poppy, as she got ready for bed. She was glad that Nicholas had enjoyed it and had liked his present. She was glad, too, that his thank-you kiss had been interrupted by other people coming into the kitchen, and that she had been able to extricate herself without completely giving away her feelings. No way was she going to let the enigmatic Dr Fordyce see how much he was affecting her. That would remain her secret, and in time she would get the better of the emotions that he had stirred up in only a few days. That way, his dislike or distrust of her wouldn't hurt.

Tomorrow she would go home and spend the day with her father, and perhaps learn how Nicholas Fordyce knew of the relationship between them. But why did it seem important to know this? It could in no way affect their working relationship, and, as there was no question of their pursuing a personal one, it shouldn't matter. Or should it?

CHAPTER SEVEN

POPPY went up to London by rail on Monday. She whisked through the house tidying up after the party, and caught the ten-twenty train to Waterloo. There she took a taxi to her home near Westminster.

Her father, tall and distinguished, looking every inch the professor that he was, met her at the elegant front door, all black enamel and brass, and paid off her taxi.

He steered her through the spacious front hall, kissed her on both cheeks, and gave her a hug.

'Lovely to have you home, darling; I can't wait to hear all your news about Princes and Paediatrics. You must be thrilled to have made it at last.'

'Oh, I am; it's wonderful, all that I knew it would be.'

'I've taken a couple of days off, barring extraordinary emergencies. Mrs M. is all geared up to produce something special, and then we can go out this afternoon, shopping perhaps, as a sort of treat for making it on to Peter Pan.' He gave her a whimsical grin, and raised his eyebrows, so that she was reminded of Nicholas. 'You would like to go shopping, I presume?' he asked, in a teasing fashion.

'Christmas shopping, lovely,' said Poppy. She smiled at her father. 'Dear Mrs M.; I must go and say hello to her.'

She thought affectionately of their housekeeper-cum-friend as she made her way through to the kitchen. Mrs M., who, since her mother's death when she was a small girl, had been like a mother to her.

It had been Mrs Morgan, affectionately referred to as Mrs M., who had understood why Poppy needed to go and train in a provincial hospital when her affair with her father's registrar had broken up. She had encouraged Poppy to get away from her father's loving but overpowering influence, and the awful possibility of being used ever again by up-and-coming medical men trying to win her father's favour through her.

Poppy, a beautiful eighteen-year-old, fresh from school, had been bowled over by the attentions of an older man, especially a man who seemed committed to her father as one of his firm. For this man, Poppy had been willing to give up her nursing ambitions, and turn her thoughts to becoming a perfect wife for a future consultant.

When her false romance ended, Poppy had applied for a place at Princes Park, without using her father's name and influence, and had been accepted, which had been a great boost to her morale.

In the kitchen, Mrs M., making pastry and up to her elbows in flour, offered a cheek for Poppy to kiss, and then sent her back to join her father in the sitting-room. 'I'm too busy to stand around chatting,' she said. 'We'll have a natter later. You go and talk to Sir Rowland; he's been missing you.'

Poppy and her father always found plenty to talk about when together; when personal matters had been discussed, there was always 'shop'.

'So you've made it at last, Poppy,' said the professor, a few minutes later, as they sat one each side of the elegant Adam fireplace, sipping pale dry sherry. 'You've made it to Paediatrics under your own steam. I'm very proud of you.' He raised his glass in a gesture of congratulations. 'Now tell me all about it. Is Sister O'Brien still in charge as she was when you were training?'

'She is,' confirmed Poppy, thinking what a prodigious memory her father had. Amazing that he remembered Rose O'Brien's name after all these years, and with all the other things he had to think about in the course of his work. They talked about Rose and about some of her small patients and their conditions.

Presently, her father asked after Ruth and Jacky, whom he'd known since they were schoolgirls. This, thought Poppy, is the point where I throw Nicholas's name into the conversation, and see whether there is any reaction.

'We had a party last night,' she said, 'Ruth and Jacky and I, to celebrate my getting on to Peter Pan, and tied it in with a birthday party for our new registrar, Nicholas Fordyce. It was great fun.'

Her father frowned. 'Fordyce,' he said thoughtfully. 'That name rings a bell.' He looked puzzled.

Poppy said as casually as she could, 'He's been up in Scotland for the last couple of years, as a registrar, and has come to Princes as a senior. I don't know what he was doing before that.'

Her father's face cleared. 'Of course, I remember, he was on my firm as a relief at one time. He was already booked for someone else, and did a fill-in job, must be four, five years ago. He was only with me a short while. I'd have liked to have kept him; he showed great promise. Well, well, so now he's at Princes with

you, my dear. Does he know that you're my daughter?
I shouldn't think that anything much escaped that
bright young man.'

'Yes, he recognised me. He didn't say how, but now
I realise that he must have seen me when I visited St
Christopher's when he was on your firm. Gracious, I
could only have been eighteen or nineteen at the time.
Fancy him remembering me.'

'Doesn't surprise me,' said her father, looking at her
affectionately. 'You're by way of being a very attractive young woman, you know. The sort of young
woman whom young men tend to notice.' He drained
his glass, and looked speculatively at his daughter,
twirling his empty glass in his fingers as he did so. 'You
can give my regards to young Fordyce when next you
see him; a bright chap, very bright chap.'

Poppy returned to Princes on Wednesday morning in
good time for afternoon duty.

Both on her journey back, and on and off over the
next few days, with her father's revelations fresh in the
mind, she thought about how Nicholas had first met
her father as a young medic. He must have been very
conscious of the professor's authority and distinction.
No wonder he was certain that her career had been
furthered by her father's influence, and not by her own
efforts.

And the fact that he was an old friend of Nina's
didn't help. He must have hoped that she'd get the
post, or at least be beaten to it fair and square. As it
was, when he'd recognised Poppy, his disappointment
had led him to suspect that she had got the job not by
merit, but by influence.

Well, at least he now knew the truth about the matter, since Nina herself had confirmed that Poppy had got the job because she was a good nurse, though he still seemed sceptical. Perhaps he had personal reasons to particularly dislike people who were successful with somebody else's help. He had sounded very bitter about influential persons in high places. But surely, after getting to know her a little at the birthday party, he wouldn't have any doubts about her right to the staffing position on the unit, and they could work together free of any resentment.

As for their personal relationship, Poppy shrugged, and resolved not to let her feelings on that score get the better of her. She would ignore the way she was beginning to feel about him, which had taken her by surprise, especially after her initial antagonism in response to his apparent dislike.

Just because Nicholas had kissed her with great warmth when he thanked her for his present, she mustn't let her imagination run away with her. It had just been a thank-you kiss, nothing more, a little emotional, of course, because of the Christmas atmosphere, and the fact that they had had a few drinks, but nothing more. If Nina hadn't gone swanning off with Dick Kendall, Nicholas would have stuck to her like glue for the evening, and the interlude in the kitchen would never have arisen. There would have been no kiss, just a laugh at the appropriateness of the gift, and a thank-you to everyone, not a special thank-you to herself.

No, she told herself fiercely, there was nothing of substance in Nicholas's attitude to suggest that he was interested in her in any but the most casual way. She must not hanker for anything more than just pleasant friendship between them.

As it turned out, even if she had wanted to do so, there really wasn't much opportunity over the next week to pursue a personal relationship with Nicholas. The children's ward, and Obstetrics and Maternity, not to mention Out-patients and the special baby unit, claimed his attention for most of the day, and much of the night. Even Nina, thought Poppy, couldn't be seeing much of him these days.

She said as much to Jacky when she got home from late duty on the Monday following her visit to see her father.

They were sitting in the warm, homely kitchen of Victoria House, shoes kicked off after a tiring day on their feet, steaming mugs of coffee before them, when Poppy voiced her thoughts.

'Poor Nina,' she said. 'She must be a bit fed up this week, with Nicholas working flat out. I bet she hasn't seen hide nor hair of him.'

Jacky stared at her friend in amazement. 'Surely,' she said, 'even you, who are the world's worst communicator when it comes to the grapevine, must have heard about Nina and Dick?'

'Nina and Dick,' repeated Poppy stupidly. 'What do you mean?'

'Well, really,' said Jacky in an exasperated tone, 'don't you notice anything? Nina and Nicholas are no longer an item.'

'Oh,' said Poppy. 'Have I missed something?' A strange sensation of hope mingled with excitement washed over her. 'What do you mean about Nina and Nicholas?'

'They've split up, finished. Nina seems to have transferred her affections to Dick Kendall; even you must have noticed that they got together at the party.'

'I thought it was just a thing that happened that evening, and would pass, and that Dick was doing the pursuing as usual, and Nina would remind him that she and Nicholas had a thing going.'

'Well, from what I've heard, it was love at first sight, you know, across a crowded room and all that.'

'Poor Nicholas,' said Poppy softly. 'He must be devastated.'

Jacky gave her an exasperated look, and snorted. 'Unlikely, but for heaven's sake, you like the guy; why don't you pick up the pieces, if there are any, and offer a shoulder to cry on? Now that all this business of your father is out of the way, you should be able to get through to the charismatic Dr Nick, who has got half the female staff drooling over him. If you don't step into the gap that Nina's left, somebody else will, and pretty damn quick.'

That night, Poppy lay awake, thinking of Nicholas. She had to admit, while trying to hang on to some vestige of pride, that she was excited at the prospect of Nicholas being a free agent, with no Nina to consider. Perhaps the thank-you kiss that he had given her on the night of the party might not have been as casual as she had thought. Maybe Nicholas had already been thinking of a future without Nina. It was impossible to tell from his enigmatic exterior.

Eventually she fell asleep, still trying to sort out her feelings for Nicholas, and his possible response to her should she dare to reveal them.

The following afternoon was hectic. Poppy was

working on the oncology unit, with the children suffering from various cancers. It was particularly harrowing
nursing there. Many of the young patients had lost
their hair as a result of their treatment, which somehow seemed to make them more vulnerable than the
other sick children. It wasn't easy to be cheerful and
jolly when you were crying inside, she thought. And it
wasn't easy to be detached either, whatever the powers
that be might say about not getting involved with
patients.

She was on late shift, and just after six o'clock a
Down's syndrome child of four was admitted from
Casualty, with all the signs and symptoms of acute
leukaemia.

Sister O'Brien was off duty, and Poppy in charge.

She decided to bleep for Nicholas. It was a gut
feeling that told her that the little patient should be
seen by him rather than the houseman who was on
call, and who would normally have attended a new
admission. Little Rosy Dawson was a very sick child,
and needed the expert attention of the most experi-
enced doctor available, and Nicholas was that doctor.
It was the sort of decision that Sister O'Brien would
have made in order to do her best for 'her children'!

Nicholas arrived just as Poppy was getting Rosy
settled in bed, and reassuring anxious parents, who
hadn't wanted to leave their daughter's side, that all
would be well.

She gave a sigh of relief as she introduced him to Mr
and Mrs Dawson, and then drew back so that he could
talk to them freely. His manner was wonderful, gentle
but firm. He was a great comfort to have around.

He looked terribly tired, Poppy thought, his long,

narrow face drawn and lined, and his dark brown eyes sunken for want of sleep. Briefly, she was sorry that she had called him, to add to his load, but only briefly. She'd had no option.

'I'm going to ask you to go to the office for a short while,' Nicholas said to Mr and Mrs Dawson, 'just while I examine Rosy, then I hope to be able to give you more information.' He turned to Poppy. 'Will you arrange for a nurse, Staff, to give Mr and Mrs Dawson tea or coffee and stay with them for a bit? You come back here, please, and help me with Rosy.'

'Of course, Doctor.'

Poppy escorted the Dawsons to the office.

'We'll look after Rosy, you know,' she said, 'all of us. And Dr Nick is marvellous with the children; he's a very gentle person, and will take good care not to frighten her. Trust him.'

She beckoned to a second-year student who was passing, and asked her to look after the Dawsons. She then collected an examination trolley and joined Nicholas by the small patient's bedside.

He was sitting on the edge of Rosy's bed, holding her hand, and talking to her quietly. Poppy knew then that she had been right to call him in. His junior would have been kind too, and would have satisfactorily dealt with the purely medical condition, but only someone of Nicholas's calibre could tap into the heart of the matter, and the heart of the child. Only someone with his experience and gentleness could get a true picture of what was happening to this already handicapped little girl without frightening her.

Nicholas smiled at both Rosy and Poppy.

'Now,' he said to the little girl, 'Nurse Poppy is

going to help me examine you, Rosy, and the first
thing that I want to do is to look into your mouth.
Your mummy tells me that your gums are sore.'

'They bleed, all bloody in my mouth this morning,'
said Rosy, her typically slanting and slightly puffy
eyelids widening.

Nicholas nodded, and said calmly, 'It can happen,
Rosy, blood in your mouth. Now can you open wide
for me?' Rosy obliged, and Poppy handed him a
spatula with which to hold down the child's tongue.
He shone a pencil torch into the little girl's mouth, and
examined it thoroughly.

When he finished, he dropped the used spatula into
the receiver that Poppy handed him, and proceeded
with the rest of his examination. He was feeling, as
Poppy knew, for raised glands behind the ears,
beneath the jaw and under the arms. He examined
Rosy's abdomen, after making her laugh by blowing
on her bare tummy.

'Liver and spleen grossly enlarged,' he murmured to
Poppy, as he motioned to her to pull the bedclothes
up over the small form. 'Not much doubt that it's acute
lymphatic leukaemia, though we'll have to do all the
usual tests to confirm. You see to Rosy——' he smiled
again at the little girl '—while I go and talk to her
parents. See what you can do to explain to her that
she will have to stay with us for a while.'

'Will do.' Poppy risked putting a hand on his arm. 'I
know you'll say the right thing,' she said, knowing that
telling parents that their child had a life-threatening or
chronic disease was heart-rending and difficult. In this
instance, with Rosy already suffering from Down's
syndrome, it would be particularly harrowing.

Nicholas covered her hand with his for a brief moment, and her own hand trembled. 'Thanks,' he said. 'I'll do my best, and thanks for calling me. You did the right thing.'

'I'm glad you understand; it seemed important that you saw her immediately.'

'It was, it is. Your instincts were right.' He smiled down at the small girl. 'Some people need extra-special care, don't they, love?' He ruffled Rosy's hair, and his eyes, soft and warm, met Poppy's as he straightened up. 'You're a splendid nurse,' he said quietly. 'We're lucky to have you here.'

Poppy felt the blood rush to her face. He was actually directly complimenting her. 'Thanks,' she said. 'It's nice to be appreciated.'

'No more than you deserve,' said Nicholas gruffly, and moved off to talk to Mr and Mrs Dawson.

Poppy, feeling elated by Nicholas's remark, set about reassuring Rosy and tidying her bed.

By the time she was ready to go off duty a few hours later she was tired, and still buoyed up by Nicholas's compliment. But it had been an emotionally wearing day, and she handed over to the night staff with relief.

It was bitterly cold, with a pale moon silvering the frost on the trees and the gravelled driveway in front of the building, when Poppy let herself out through the front entrance. She was walking briskly through the car park towards her car when she heard swift, long strides behind her. She recognised the footsteps as belonging to Nicholas. She slowed down, and half turned, and he caught her up at once.

'Going home?' he asked, putting a casual hand on her arm.

'Yes, and looking forward to it—a hot drink, hot bath and bed,' said Poppy, keeping her voice steady, and trying not to respond too obviously to the touch of his hand. Surely he must feel her pulses bounding.

'Pity,' he said. 'I was hoping that you would come and have a drink with me.'

'I don't drink and drive, Doctor,' she said stiffly, not meaning to be stiff. It was nerves, of course, because he was touching her and was standing so close.

'I said a drink; it doesn't have to be intoxicating,' said Nicholas, evenly. 'It could be anything. It was your company I was seeking, not an excuse to get you legless.'

The teasing tone in his voice made Poppy feel incredibly mean and silly.

'I'm sorry, I rather jumped to conclusions.' She made herself relax, and said with a grin, 'I'd love to have a non-intoxicating drink with you. Where?'

'Poachers?'

'Fine, I should like that.'

'We'll have to drive separately; I'm still on call.'

'That's fine by me.' Poppy by now had reached her car. She opened the door. 'See you there in a few minutes,' she said.

'Great,' said Nicholas as he climbed into the Range Rover. 'I'll follow you down.'

Poppy's thoughts were chaotic as she drove down the mile-long drive to the inn. Did Nicholas want to see her because Nina had let him down, or did he want to see her for herself? Or was he affected by the friendly exchange on the ward, and their combined efforts with little Rosy Dawson? She felt a mounting excitement at the thought of being with him. All her

nerve-endings tingled in anticipation. It would be the
first time that they had been alone together socially
since their tête-à-tête in the kitchen on the night of the
party.

She wondered if Nicholas was thinking that too,
and, if he was, how it was affecting him. Would he
refer to it? Would he be embarrassed either about the
incident or because at the time he was escorting Nina?
Well, she would soon know; they were almost at
Poachers.

She turned into the wide sweep of drive in front of
the elegant Georgian façade of the old coaching-inn,
with its porticoed entrance. She had come here often
over the years with other Princes staff, who used the
rather up-market hotel as their local, but never on
previous occasions, even happy ones, with such a
strong feeling that something special was going to
happen.

It's ludicrous, she told herself. What could possibly
happen that could make an invitation to have a drink
with a colleague, even a colleague like Nicholas
Fordyce, all that special?

Nicholas drove in and parked beside her, and was
out of the Range Rover, and standing at the door of
her car, by the time she had released her belt, and
picked up her shoulder-bag from the passenger seat.
He held the door open for her and after she had locked
it took her arm, and steered her towards the front
door of the hotel. Her bones turned to water at his
touch. She felt limp with longing for this lean, handsome man who was striding along beside her. She
turned her head to look at him. Was the same thing
happening to him? Did his feelings match hers? No,

he seemed as calm and in control as ever. Nothing about him indicated that he was experiencing any of the emotions that were threatening to overwhelm her.

'My word, it's cold,' he said, as they reached the lamplit portico. 'The sooner we get something hot to drink and find a nice warm spot to sit, the better, don't you agree?' He smiled down at her, and pulled her a little closer. His eyes were dark pools in the lamplight, his hand squeezed her arm, and all her nerves pulsed in response. The pressure of his hand, and the nearness of his strong body, sent waves of sensuous pleasure washing over her.

'I certainly do,' she murmured faintly, and shivered, and prayed that he would think that she was simply feeling the cold. She was still anxious that he shouldn't realise how positively she was reacting to him; it was too soon. They were only just getting to know each other, and such strong emotions had no place in a relationship that was still full of uncertainties, still getting off the ground. She must remind herself that this was just an invitation to share a drink, not an invitation to a night of unbridled passion. She swallowed a nervous giggle at the thought, and shivered again.

'Poor girl, you're frozen.' They reached the large, heavy front door, and Nicholas thrust it open, and pushed her gently inside. 'But you'll be all right now. This is lovely and warm; you'll soon thaw out.'

He smiled down at her again, and this time, in the stronger light of the high-ceilinged reception area, with its magnificent chandelier all ablaze, she could see a warm glow in his brown eyes.

Reception, decked out in Christmas finery, with

holly and other evergreens, was empty, and the doors to the lounge bar and hotel rooms were closed, though a murmur of voices could be heard from the bar.

Nicholas turned Poppy round to face him, and then put a hand under her chin to tilt her head upwards. 'Look,' he whispered, 'somebody's put mistletoe in the chandelier.'

Poppy stared upwards, and there, much to her surprise, she saw that Nicholas was right, for, woven in and around the electric candles of the magnificent centre lighting piece, were the creamy waxen berries and dull olive-green leaves of branches of mistletoe.

She lowered her gaze, and managed a light laugh. 'I didn't think that Poachers went in for that sort of thing,' she said. 'They're too up-market.' Her voice was breathless; his eyes were boring into hers, and she couldn't look away.

'I don't see why not,' said Nicholas, sliding his hands down her arms and linking them behind her back at waist-level. 'It's a much older custom than the Christmas tree, lads kissing the lasses under the mistletoe. It dates back to the Druids, I believe, the veneration of the shrub.' He pulled her close. 'Don't you think it would be a shame to ignore such an ancient custom?' he asked softly. 'It would be an awful waste of good mistletoe.' Poppy continued to look up at him uncertainly, longing for him to kiss her, and yet not quite sure whether she should let it happen. 'Poppy. . .' His voice dropped to a husky drawl, though there was a firmness in it that was hard to ignore. 'I want to kiss you quite badly, and you want to kiss me, don't you?'

His hands on her back were pressing her even closer,

and she could feel his body against hers, hard and demanding. She could smell his aftershave and the masculine scent of his skin. His eyes gleamed; they seemed to devour her. She put her hands round his neck and pushed her fingers through his thick brown hair.

'Yes, I do,' she whispered, 'very much.' She lifted her face for him to kiss.

His mouth came down slowly on hers, and met her lips gently at first, and then, as he felt her responding to him, with a greater urgency, a greater demand. His tongue probed her lips, parting them with little darting movements, until she opened her mouth, and let him explore her moist softness, capitulating with a little moan of pleasure to his tongue's demands. For minutes they remained locked together until they heard somebody opening the door of the lounge bar.

Reluctantly they pulled apart, breathing heavily, though Nicholas kept his arm round her waist. He nodded to the departing customers and guided Poppy towards the door of the bar. 'Thank you,' he said softly, giving her a brilliant smile as they passed into the crowded room. 'That was a wonderful Christmas present.' He bent his head a little lower, and whispered in her ear, 'I hope that you enjoyed the experience as much as I did.'

Poppy nodded. She was shaking and incapable of speech.

The people who had just left the bar had vacated seats on an old-fashioned high-backed bench beside the roaring log fire. Nicholas took Poppy's hand, and led her there, threading his way round the tables in the crowded room. There were quite a few Princes people present, with whom they exchanged greetings as they moved to their table. Seeing some of the looks that were being directed towards them, Poppy made a half-hearted attempt to withdraw her hand from Nicholas's, but he only took a firmer grip on it, and smiled at her.

He sat her down on the settee, and said with a grin and a decidedly wicked gleam in his eye, 'Too late, my dear girl, to pretend that we're just good friends. The grapevine, I think you will find, has already decreed otherwise.'

Poppy smiled back at him shyly. She wished that the grapevine were correct for once, for now she knew without a doubt that she would like to be more than just good friends with Nicholas. She gathered her scattered wits. 'I'm not sure,' she said brightly, 'that we can even be classed as good friends, as, except for the party, we've hardly spoken to each other on personal terms.' She looked up at him through her long lashes as he bent over the table, and almost added that he'd been anything but friendly, until now. But she couldn't bring herself to say this; there was a look in his eyes that prevented her.

'Well, we can soon remedy that,' he said, his voice very firm and authoritative. 'We'll talk about it when I come back with the drinks. What will you have?'

Poppy asked for tea with lemon, but when Nicholas returned he was carrying a tray with four glasses on it — two teas and two other glasses containing a steaming amber-coloured liquid.

'The hotel's produced a driver's special,' he explained, 'made up of hot fruit juices and various spices. Smells delicious; I thought we should try a glass.'

'Lovely,' Poppy said as she buried her neat little *retroussée* nose in the glass.

'Yes,' murmured Nicholas, 'I second that.' But he was looking not at the drink, but at Poppy's shining head bent over the glass.

Poppy took a sip of the drink. 'Oh, yummy,' she said. 'I could get hooked on this.'

She raised her head and looked sideways at Nicholas sitting beside her. Their eyes met, and this time there was no mistaking the admiration that she saw in his. Admiration, and something more. Was it just naked desire, sparked off by their sensuous kiss, or could it be love. . .or something very like love?

CHAPTER EIGHT

NICHOLAS had only just sat down at the table and taken a sip of his drink when his bleeper sounded.

He pulled a face at Poppy. 'I might have known,' he said. 'Sorry about this.' He touched her lightly on the arm before getting up to go to the bar phone.

'Well, it's to be expected; you are on call,' said Poppy, trying to keep her voice steady, trying to sound detached, conscious of the spot where he had touched her, conscious of a rising excitement as she watched him go to the bar. She struggled with a tangle of emotions that she couldn't sort out. She wanted to be with him; she didn't want to be with him. She wanted him to touch her again, and yet a small part of her was afraid of what would happen if he did touch her. She felt breathless, and tried to slow her breathing down by taking long, deep breaths.

Everything was happening so fast. She wanted time to think. There was something like relief, mixed with disappointment, as she realised that the evening looked like being cut short before it had properly begun.

She wasn't sure that she could handle the situation right now. The sheer intensity and sensuality of Nicholas's kiss had surprised her, and the fact that she had been so aroused by it, and responded in the same fashion, surprised her even more.

Tentatively she touched her lips which his had so

fiercely touched. They felt tender, slightly swollen, slightly sore. She ran the tip of her tongue over them, and shivered at the memory of that delightful, thrilling and utterly abandoned kiss under the mistletoe, when they had melted into each other, thighs and hips touching as their kissing got deeper and deeper.

She shivered, and suddenly her mind was filled with memories of the past. Never had she been kissed like that before, not even by Jeremy Franks, her ex-fiancé. But then she had been barely eighteen, and she had thought that Jeremy's cool kisses were the norm. Only later, when the true reason for his interest in her had emerged, had she guessed that he had been cold because he didn't care. He hadn't loved her. He had simply been using her as a stepping-stone in his promotion stakes. If the offer from America hadn't arrived, they would have married. The awful thought made her shudder. Just imagine being married to the dreadful Jeremy, whose sophistication had swept her off her feet, and whose apparent dedication to his work had deceived even her usually perceptive father.

Thinking of all this now, in the warm friendliness of Poachers, with Nicholas using the telephone only yards away, Poppy realised that the experience had made her unconsciously wary of men for a long time, and since then she had had only the occasional light-hearted relationship. She had taken pride in the fact that she was far more interested in her career than in men, and a serious affair was just not on; it was the last thing she wanted.

No wonder she was having mixed feelings now, and wasn't sure how she wanted to respond to Nicholas, and the extraordinary sensations he was arousing. She wasn't even sure that she could resist him, but everything about her past told her to be cautious. She would proceed carefully with the charismatic Nicholas. No way was she going to fall into the trap that she had with Jeremy Franks all those years ago, in spite of the way he had just kissed her, and sent her senses reeling.

Nicholas returned to the table and put an end to her rambling thoughts. He didn't even bother to sit down, just reached for a glass and took a swallow of tea.

'I've got to go,' he said, 'at once, I'm afraid. It's a baby in the special unit. So sorry.' He put a hand on her shoulder and squeezed it gently. She felt that she was burning where he touched her, and was furious with herself for being so affected, when he seemed so casual. There was no hint now of the passionate man of a few minutes earlier. 'Thank you for the beginnings of what might have been a lovely evening.' He gave her a quirky grin. 'Who knows, Poppy, where it would have ended, if things had turned out differently, and I'd not got called away.'

As he smiled, her heart seemed to give an almost physical, painful jump. His dark brown eyes bored into hers, conveying all sorts of unspoken messages. She felt herself blushing and going hot all over as she digested what he seemed to be saying with his lips, and what he was saying with his eyes.

Was he suggesting that they might have gone far beyond the kissing stage as the evening progressed? She couldn't be sure, and wished that she could read him better. She dropped her eyes, unable to meet his compelling gaze any longer, sure that he, at any rate, could read her every thought. Perhaps, those same thoughts rushed on in a wave of excitement, he meant that they could go on to make love in his flat in Eton House. The idea of being alone with him, and receiving more passionate kisses of the sort that he had given her under the mistletoe, made her already galloping pulses race faster. Her whole body suddenly ached with a longing to be crushed against his hard body; she could imagine his hands exploring, coaxing. . .

Something like common sense took over. This was the responsible Nicholas Fordyce she was thinking of, whom she was building fantasies around in spite of her determination not to become too involved, not some crass young houseman out for a bit of fun. He wouldn't expect to rush her into bed; not on a first casual date, not before they had got to know each other better. He was too sophisticated, too mature for that. He wouldn't be into one-night stands any more than she was, in spite of his reputation for attracting every female within miles. Surely his words, and the unspoken messages that he conveyed with his eyes, simply meant that they would have begun that process of getting to know each other, and nothing more.

She smiled, a little uncertainly, and he put a forefinger beneath her chin and tilted her head so that she was looking full at him again. He must have read her mind, as she had suspected, for he used the very words that had been in her thoughts, as he said softly but firmly, 'A great pity that we haven't time tonight to get to know each other better. I think the experience would have been, to say the least, interesting.' He shook his head slightly, and looked quizzically at her, bringing his well marked eyebrows together in a frown. 'Just as well, probably, that it's not possible. Who would have thought that you were so vulnerable, so unsophisticated, beneath all that style?' He paused for a moment and smiled at her again. 'Well, another time, perhaps. Goodnight, my dear.' He brushed a light kiss across her forehead, raised a hand in farewell, and left.

Poppy watched him confidently shouldering his way through a crowd of people who had just come into her bar. His height made his head still visible above everyone else as he made his way to the door. She wondered if he might look back again and wave before he disappeared through it, but he didn't.

In bed that night, Poppy, in an agony of uncertainty, went over and over the events of the evening, from that long, passionate, melting kiss that had welded them together, to Nicholas's rather cool and enigmatic farewell remark. He had seemed to read her mind so accurately in those last few minutes before he left, guessing that she was unsure of herself and had reservations about how to proceed. He'd also decided that she was childishly innocent, though he'd politely called it vulnerable, but that was what he'd meant, and he'd confirmed it by saying that she was unsophisticated.

His last remark hadn't been exactly dismissive, but it had implied that there might not be any point in continuing with their fragile relationship, so unlike the bold, easy affair that he must have had with Nina. He was not the sort of man to take advantage of a woman, and he probably thought that that was what he would be doing if he fostered a relationship with her. Which meant, surely, that he couldn't feel about her the way she did about him, or he wouldn't be able to hold back. Did his heart jump when he saw her, or even heard her voice, as hers did when she saw or heard him? Did her touch linger on him, as his did on her?

She could have wept, and almost did, burying her hot face in the pillow, and biting her tender lips hard, in order to stop the tears.

She told herself that it would not be the end of the world if she and Nicholas didn't see each other again, except at work, but the awful emptiness as she envisaged the thought was frightening. It made her feel hollow. In a couple of weeks, Nicholas Fordyce had become important to her, and not just as a colleague or her boss. When he was near by, it was all she could do not to reach out and touch him, and tonight, when they had come off duty, she was sure that he had felt the same. It was as if they had been drawn together by an invisible thread, a thread that had pulled them finally together in that long, passionate kiss.

All her preconceived ideas, based on her broken engagement to Jeremy, about remaining aloof from a demanding relationship collapsed. She desperately wanted to get to know Nicholas better — he was, she knew, the only man she would ever want to get to know in depth — but the way she had bungled things tonight made it unlikely that she would ever get the chance. She had revealed herself for what she was — a naïve, over-sensitive young woman, incapable, probably, of pleasing an authoritative, sophisticated man like Nicholas.

No wonder he had seemed dismissive, almost, about their getting to know each other better. He had decided that she was an innocent child, and not a mature woman, and had lost interest. She had blown it, by letting him see that she was half scared of carrying on from where their kiss had finished. She still thought that he wouldn't have pushed too far on their first date, because it didn't go with the cool, detached streak that Nicholas had in him, but he must have been expecting some sort of response from her that would tell him that she would be, in time, ready and willing for anything. Now, it seemed, she had even failed in that. Some deep-seated innocence, or fear left over from the past, held her back. He was right about her being vulnerable. She was vulnerable; she couldn't bear the thought of repeating the hurt of years ago.

At last she fell into an uneasy sleep, from which she awoke just before her alarm clock sounded, feeling like nothing on earth.

She put on rather more make-up than usual to disguise the shadows beneath her eyes, and set off for work, rigid with determination not to let last night's events affect her in any way. She would play it cool with Nicholas when she met him, let him see that she was in command of herself, that she was not the unsophisticated girl that he seemed to think her. Yes, she determined as she went on duty, she would make him see that he was wrong in his assessment of her last night; she would be haughty and rather remote, and that would make him think again.

As always, it was easy while work absorbed her to set aside all her peculiar personal thoughts, and her decision about how she would react towards Nicholas gave her a kind of courage which cheered her. All was not lost; she would just have to find a fresh way to capture his interest.

The ward was busy, with all beds occupied, many by

children who could be given minor operations and be discharged before Christmas, now just over a week away. This would be the last intake, barring emergencies, before the holiday.

The older children in the play-room were being encouraged to make glittery decorations for Peter Pan, where a Christmas tree would be erected in a couple of days' time. A platform was to be put up at the end of the ward, so that the tree would be out of reach of small, inquisitive fingers. The decoration of the tree would be left to the unit staff.

'I always try to make a little party of tree-decorating day,' Sister O'Brien told Poppy, and the other nurses on duty, 'involving the children, and the staff — medical and nursing — and any visitors who are here. It makes it more bearable for those who have to remain in over Christmas, and a jolly day for those going home. People are very generous, and we get no end of packages left round the tree in those last few days for the children who are going to be here over Christmas.'

'Do they have a Father Christmas come round?' asked one of the students.

'Always,' said Sister. 'Usually one of the doctors, but, failing that, one of the League of Friends.'

'Do we know who is going to be Father Christmas this year, Sister?' asked the other student.

'Yes, a real prize this time. Dr Nick has offered to be Santa Claus, since he's officially off for part of Christmas Day. He and the junior reg are sharing duties between them.'

That figures, thought Poppy. He would offer to do just that. What a kind man he is when it comes to the children; nothing's too much trouble for them. There's nothing enigmatic about his response to his patients, whatever he's like with me. As soon as the thought rose, she tried to squash it. She must stop thinking of him as being perfect; he wasn't. After all, she thought, he's a bachelor, and, now that he has finished with Nina, what else would he do on Christmas Day? It's not really much of a sacrifice for him to give up the day to the children.

With difficulty Poppy wrenched her mind back from her irritating thoughts to listen to Sister's instructions for the rest of the morning. One of the students present was to supervise the play-room. Poppy was to take the other student to prep the patients listed for surgery later in the morning, the early children for Theatre having already been prepped by the night staff.

'Here's the list, Staff,' said Sister, handing her a slip of paper with the names of children for operations. 'By the time you finish getting them ready and giving them their pre-med injections, some of the early ones should be on their way back from Recovery, and you can keep Nurse with you to organise their post-op care.'

'Yes, Sister,' said Poppy, quickly taking the list from her senior, anxious to get on with her work and put Nicholas Fordyce out of her mind for a few hours.

There was little chance of his coming to the ward for some time, as he must have already made his round of the children who were due for surgery while the night staff were on. From now on, he would be busy in Theatre for much of the day, so with luck she wouldn't have to face him for quite a while.

At that very moment he appeared, surprising, pleasing and dismaying her all at once. He was in theatre greens, which somehow made him look taller and thinner than ever, but they also made him look more handsome, and rugged at the same time, a curious combination. His whole bearing was one of strength and decisiveness, a man who knew where he was going, and what he was about. There was a mask dangling from his neck, which Poppy knew, from past experience, he would use to show the children what he would look like when he was operating on them. He usually made quite a little game of partly covering his face, and winking at the children above the mask. Mostly this had the desired effect of reassuring the young patients, so that they went to the theatre drowsy from their pre-medication and in a reasonably relaxed state.

Poppy felt herself go pink with her mixed emotions at the sight of him. All her good intentions flew out of the window, and she had a job not to grin inanely, as, gathering all her courage, she went forward to meet him as he stood in the doorway, smiling round at the ward full of children.

'Good morning, Doctor,' she said as formally as she could manage, trying hard to be cool and professional.

'Morning, Staff Nurse,' he replied equally formal. 'I've been busy, couldn't get in earlier, so I've come to see my young customers now.'

Several children in nearby beds giggled, and Nicholas pulled a face at them. 'Now who's at the head of the queue, Staff? Who needs my services first?' His dark brown eyes met Poppy's as he spoke, and she saw that they were full of a gentle humour, as if, she thought, he was including her in his question. Had he really seen through her? Did he really know how much she needed him?

His magnetism was unnerving. She tore her eyes away from his, and said quietly, 'Tracy Watts, adenoidectomy, she's first on the list, followed by Mark Bowles, another adenoidectomy. They've both had their pre-med.'

'Right.' He strode over to the two beds, which were side by side, and stood between them. 'Feeling sleepy?' he asked.

They both murmured that yes, they were.

In a soft, low voice he said, 'When you next see me, I'll probably look like this.' He held the mask up to his face, covering his nose. 'And so will everyone else in Theatre; that's so that we don't breathe germs all over you, OK?'

Both the children mumbled, 'OK,' and Nicholas patted each of their heads, concealed beneath theatre caps. 'Good, see you later,' he said and moved on to the next bed on Poppy's list.

And so it continued until he had seen every child on the list for the day. Always, it seemed to Poppy, he had the right word at the right time, comforting the tearful or fretful children, and joking with the more robust little patients, who amazingly seemed unperturbed by the experience that they were about to undergo.

He turned to leave, and Poppy saw him politely to the door as etiquette demanded, but when she would have turned to go he detained her, laying a hand on her arm.

'Poppy. . .' His voice, though barely above a whisper, was firm. 'We must meet, to make up for last night. When are you off duty?'

'I — I'm off at five,' she stammered, surprised, after her dismal thoughts, that he should want to see her again so soon.

'Hell, I won't be finished by then, and after that I'll be on call. What about tomorrow?'

'I'm on lates; I'll be finished at nine.'

'Right; God willing, I'll be able to get away for an hour at least. I'll pick you up in Reception at nine-fifteen, OK?'

'I'll try to make it by then.' So much for being aloof; she had a job to keep her voice steady. She felt as if she were floating several feet off the ground.

'Good.' He smiled, one of his lop-sided smiles that made her feel weak all over. Then he turned away and, without so much as a backward glance, marched down the corridor, his mind already, Poppy guessed, on the patient waiting for him in Theatre.

The following evening, after two frantically busy days on the ward, when Poppy, head in the clouds, had fought an almost losing battle to keep her mind on the job, she was ready to leave at nine, after handing over to her counterpart on night duty.

The euphoria at the thought of seeing Nicholas again, off duty, had kept her going all through the afternoon and evening and was still with her as she tidied up in the cloakroom. She changed into the narrow-legged brown velvet trousers and a cashmere sweater that she had brought with her that morning, and exchanged her sensible duty shoes for high-heeled black leather boots. Quickly she ran a comb through her shining hair, freshened her lipstick and eyeshadow, lightly dusted her face with powder, and was ready. She didn't feel in the least bit tired, although the amount of work they had all got through on the ward had left everybody else flagging.

Nicholas was waiting for her in Reception as promised. It was twenty past nine. He was leaning against the desk talking to the receptionist when she first caught sight of him, and he had his back to her, but he seemed to sense that she was coming down the stairs, and turned to watch her descend the last few steps.

Poppy hesitated five steps from the bottom of the stairs. Stupidly, she felt almost faint when she saw Nicholas waiting there. It was unbelievable that he was waiting for her. It was too good to be true, after being so sure that he wouldn't want to see her again. The lights of the tall Christmas tree, standing in the large well of the stairs, sparkled on his thick brown hair. She held on to the banister rail, and stared down as he started to move across the hall.

She watched him, mesmerised, as he strode towards the foot of the stairs. Was this sophisticated, worldly-wise man who could have the pick of the hospital really going to take her out? Did he really want to see her again? Heart in her mouth, she came to a sudden standstill, unable to put one foot in front of the other. She felt frozen to the spot. This is ridiculous, she told herself, but still she couldn't move.

'Well, hello there,' he said, sounding friendly, casual. 'Hope you haven't been too rushed; I know how busy you've been on the ward today.'

Poppy registered the fact that the night receptionist was looking at them with barely concealed curiosity, and it spurred her into action. The grapevine, after her meeting with Nicholas in Poachers, must already be busy with speculation, but there was no need to add fuel to the fire.

'Hi,' she said, and somehow made her voice sound cheerful and normal, to match his. 'Haven't kept you waiting, I hope.' She put her foot down on to the next step, caught the heel of her boot on the tread above, and went tumbling down the last few steps.

Nicholas must have moved like lightning, for he was there to catch her and stop her falling full length on the floor. He held her for a moment in strong arms, and then lowered her gently into a sitting position on the bottom step, keeping his arms round her, crouching down beside her.

Poppy's first thought was how fantastically exciting it was to have his arms around her, and her second that her right ankle hurt like hell.

'Oh, no,' she muttered, through lips tight with pain. 'I think I've damaged my ankle.'

'Which one?' His arms tightened round her for a moment.

'The right.'

'I'd better have a look. Don't want it to swell up inside your boot, or we'll never get it off.' Nicholas released his hold on her, knelt down on one knee, and raised her right foot so that it was resting on his other knee. 'Now,' he said, 'I'm going to ease it off as carefully as I can. You keep your foot as still as possible.' He took hold of the toe and heel of the boot, and pulled gently.

Poppy stifled a gasp of pain and tried to keep her foot still, as Nicholas had instructed.

'All over,' he said briskly, as he pulled the boot free. 'Now let's see what damage you've done.' He bent over, and ran sensitive fingers over her ankle, which already felt as if it was swelling. He tried to peer through the thin black silk. 'Stockings or tights?' he asked.

'Stockings.'

'Can you manage to get this one off?'

'Yes, but. . .' She looked around Reception, empty at that moment, except for the receptionist, but likely to be busy with people passing through at any moment.

'You're quite right,' said Nicholas. 'Not the best place to carry out an examination. Put your arms round my neck; I'm going to carry you through to the office behind Reception.'

'But——'

'No buts; I'm going to look at this ankle and if necessary take you to Casualty. If it doesn't need their expert attention, I'll fix it with a support bandage. That's if you trust me to make a diagnosis.' He smiled at her, and at the same time bent and scooped her up in his arms, and she, as he had instructed, put her arms round his neck.

She could smell his aftershave, as her face inevitably pressed close to his, and see the way that his longish brown hair nudged his collar. 'Oh, I do,' she murmured. 'I trust you implicitly.'

'Good girl,' he said softly, his brown eyes, so near her own, tender with compassion. 'Now if Mrs Tasker will kindly open the door to the office, we'll have a look at the offending joint.'

Mrs Tasker said rather apprehensively, 'Shouldn't

Nurse go straight to Casualty, Doctor? All staff accidents have to be reported in the book.'

'Yes, of course, I appreciate that, but I think you'll find that as long as a member of staff is seen by a senior doctor for diagnosis and simple treatment there's no problem. I'll take responsibility. Just give me time to decide whether Poppy needs to have an X-ray, and go through official channels; if not I'll sign your book to confirm treatment. OK?'

Mrs Tasker visibly relaxed. 'OK, Doctor, whatever you say.'

She let them into a fair-sized office, furnished with two desks and chairs, typewriters and several filing-cabinets.

Nicholas deposited Poppy on to a swivel chair behind one of the desks. 'Now,' he said, 'if you can undo your stocking, my dear, I'll have a proper look at this foot.' He sounded as he did when he talked to patients or relatives, firm, but reassuring.

'I'll have to undo my suspenders,' said Poppy in a small voice. She suddenly felt depressed and vulnerable. The whole evening had been spoilt because of her fall. By now they should have been on their way out. But since it had happened, and she needed attention, she didn't want Nicholas to treat her as he did other people; she wanted him to look on her as someone special, not just any patient.

Common sense told her that she was being irrational. He was treating her as a patient because that was what she was at this moment. At least he had insisted on looking at her ankle himself and hadn't whisked her off to Casualty as Mrs Tasker had suggested. But even the pleasure of having Nicholas concerned for her didn't make her feel much better. He must think her such a fool for spoiling his precious time off.

She looked tentatively at his face and was surprised to find him smiling widely. He didn't look cross, or even irritated. His eyes twinkled.

'Can I help?' he asked, stretching out a hand as if to help undo her trousers. 'I'm good with buttons and things.'

'Don't you dare,' she said, and laughed. At once her depression disappeared. He had teased her into a good humour, just as surely as he sometimes teased his small patients, but he had managed, too, to inject a personal note into his teasing, so that she did feel special, just as she had hoped.

Once she had freed her stocking, Nicholas, sitting on the other swivel chair, raised her right leg on to his knees, and, pushing up the narrow leg of her trousers over her slender calf, began his examination. Gently his fingers moved over the pale, stretched skin of her fast-swelling ankle, as he watched her face for signs of pain.

'Can you wiggle your toes?' he asked.

Poppy obediently did so.

'Does it hurt here, or here, when you do so?' He touched a couple of spots near her ankle bone.

'No.'

'Good. I'm sure you haven't broken anything; it's a straightforward sprain, and, the sooner I get it band-aged up, the better.' He stroked her foot lightly, massaging upward from the toes.

Poppy shivered at his touch, unable to stop herself, and Nicholas frowned.

'Does that hurt?' he asked, sounding surprised.

'No, it's not that. Someone walked over my grave, I expect,' she invented quickly.

'Really.' He looked as if he didn't believe her, but whether he suspected her true reason for shivering she couldn't tell, for his face gave nothing away. 'Well, you're not in or near the grave yet, my dear girl. I'm going to nip along to the nearest ward and pinch a support bandage. You'll feel fine once that's on.' He leaned forward and kissed her on the tip of her nose. 'Don't go away,' he said. 'I'll be back with the necessary in a couple of minutes.'

Poppy sat in a happy daze while he was gone. His kiss, though casual and unsexy, paternal almost, made her feel warm and wanted, and the fact that he didn't appear to be cross about her accident cheered her immensely. She looked at her watch. In spite of all that had happened, it was only just after nine-thirty. They still had time to enjoy a drink and a chat.

True to his word, Nicholas was back within a very short time, not only with a tubigrip bandage, and a plastic bag full of crushed ice, but an elbow crutch.

'You see,' he said with a smile, 'I come bearing gifts from the rehab unit. One of the physios was on duty and was only too happy to supply all our needs.'

Your needs, thought Poppy a trifle sourly. Whoever was there did it for you, not for me.

'But I don't need a crutch,' she said. 'I shall be able to walk quite well once my ankle's bandaged.'

'Yes, limp around and do even more damage, when you don't have to. Come on, don't be a silly girl; give your ankle a chance to heal.' He lifted her leg from the chair and sat himself down as before, with her foot resting on his knee, and proceeded to bind the ice pack in place with a cotton bandage, before securing it with the stretchy shaped bandage.

She relaxed, and watched his hands at work on her foot, and thought how beautiful they were, so strong, and yet so gentle. She imagined them caressing her, and a smile hovered round her lips. She wanted to reach out and touch the gleaming head bent over her injured limb. She was glad that this had happened, for surely it had brought them closer. There was no antagonism in Nicholas now, just warmth and affection.

He looked up and found her smiling at him. 'Nearly finished,' he murmured, 'then we'll go and have a bite to eat and something to drink and I'll take you home.'

'I've got my car.'

'You can't drive tonight with your ankle as it is. I'll drive you back, and pick you up in the morning. By tomorrow evening you'll be all right.'

'But——'

'No buts, I mean it.'

'Now look here, you can't order me around.' She felt suddenly mutinous.

'Oh, but I can, both as a doctor and your boss, and someone who cares what happens to you. Do you think that I would let you drive on a freezing cold night on a treacherous road with a gammy ankle?'

Their eyes clashed, Poppy's full of rebellion at being ordered around, and Nicholas's with a determined glint in them.

She opened her mouth to protest further, but he laid a finger on her lips, and shook his head.

'Enough,' he said firmly, forbidding her to argue

any more. 'There, I've finished.' He slipped her stocking over her bandaged foot, rolled it neatly, and pulled her trouser leg down. 'No chance of putting your boot on; you'll have to hop. Now let's get out of here and try to relax for an hour or so.'

CHAPTER NINE

POPPY saw very little of Nicholas over the next few days. He had his hands full, not only on Peter Pan, but on the other units for which he was responsible, all of which were particularly busy just before Christmas. Because of her sprained ankle she was working in the baby cubicles, where feeding and bathing the infants could be carried out sitting down.

As she was working alone, she had time to think. She mulled over again and again the events of the evening she had spent with Nicholas, which had started with such promise, in spite of her fall down the stairs.

Nicholas had made her feel special, and even rather precious, when he was treating her ankle. His hands and eyes had been gentle, intimate, and had seemed to promise great things for the evening ahead, yet once the interlude was over he'd changed. He was cheerful and friendly but nothing more.

They had sat thigh to thigh in the crowded pub, eating and drinking, and she had been conscious of his nearness the whole time, with her pulses bumping like mad, and her breathing erratic. Whether he felt the same, she had no idea. Occasionally she had caught him looking at her with a strange expression in his eyes that made her more breathless than ever. He had seemed on the point of saying something, but hadn't.

When she had received his surprise invitation, she'd hoped that he might show some of the passion with

which he had kissed her under the mistletoe, or at
least a special pleasure in her company, but he hadn't
done that either.

The evening had fizzled out, leaving her feeling flat
and despondent, and wondering what she had done to
spoil it. He'd taken her home after the pleasant but
puzzling interlude in the pub, kissed her a friendly
goodnight on the doorstep, and had refused her offer
of coffee.

She had spent a restless and unhappy night thinking
about what might have been, and where she had gone
wrong yet again. The following morning he had picked
her up to take her to work as promised. He seemed
preoccupied, and, after enquiring after her ankle, had
made spasmodic conversation on their short journey.
They had parted politely, almost like strangers.

The more she turned all this over in her mind, the
stronger grew her conviction that Nicholas was still
suspicious as to how she had got her posting to Peter
Pan, and was holding it against her. Though why, if
that was the case, he had bothered to ask her out and
kiss her passionately was a mystery. Was it because he
was still in love with Nina, in spite of his seeming
indifference when she and Dick got together, and was
trying to make her jealous? She couldn't believe that
he was that small-minded, and, if he was, there were
plenty of other women around whom he could have
escorted.

Sadly, Poppy pushed these thoughts from her mind
and concentrated on Baby Wakely, now well nour-
ished and contented, and due to go home the following
day. She settled him in his cot.

'Now, my lad, you go to sleep; Nurse Poppy's off to

help with the Christmas tree decorations. You'll be big enough next year to join in the fun, but this year ——'

'This year he'll probably get fed turkey and Christmas pudding,' said Nicholas's voice from the doorway, 'if his mother's past form is anything to go by.'

Poppy's heart lurched. She felt herself go hot, and kept her head down over the baby, so that Nicholas wouldn't see her blushing. She must play it cool.

'At least,' she heard herself saying, with a tinge of bitterness, 'his mother is a loving mum, even though she's ignorant — and she wants him home for Christmas.'

She was surprised at how bitter she suddenly felt towards Nicholas. A great wave of anger and unhappiness washed over her. He had spoilt everything. He had spoilt her first Christmas on Children's. He had made her aware of him as she had never been aware of a man before, and had spoiled that by his indifference. She regretted that she'd ever met him, and for a fraction of a moment she even regretted having beaten his precious Nina to the Peter Pan job. If that hadn't happened, Nicholas might have loved her, instead of hating her.

She forced herself to look up at him, and found, to her surprise, that his brown eyes were gentle and kindly, not hostile or cold, as she had expected them to be.

He said softly, 'Yes, love is a strange and wonderful thing, isn't it? And it comes in all sorts of disguises to all sorts of people at any time in life.'

Poppy nodded and looked down at the sleeping baby. 'Yes,' she said, 'it does.' Her anger was ebbing away; she felt only sadness at her love having lost out before it had been acknowledged. She bent over and stroked back a strand of hair from the tiny cheek.

Nicholas moved further into the cubicle and stood beside her by the cot. For a brief, heart-stopping moment she thought that he was going to touch her, but he didn't. He just stood and stared down at the infant, his long, narrow face soft with compassion. Then he sighed and said, in his usual cool, professional voice, 'Well, Staff, I was going to examine this young man as he's going home tomorrow, but now that you've got him settled I'll leave it till later.'

Poppy swallowed. 'Thank you, Doctor, it would be a shame to disturb him now. Are there any other babes that you want to see?'

He shook his head, and his eyes were quite undreadable. 'No, no, thank you. I'll come back later.'

He turned and walked out of the cubicle without a backward glance. Poppy watched him through the glass panels as he walked down the ward, and out through the doors to the corridor.

For the rest of the day, on and off between attending to the patients, Poppy and all the staff and any visitors who were around helped with decorating the Christmas tree. True to her word, Sister O'Brien made it into a sort of party, with sausage rolls and mince pies and fizzy soft drinks for the helpers set out in the office, with a tape playing festive music.

The tree took shape by the middle of the afternoon, glittering frostily beneath the ward lights, multi-coloured tinsel and baubles twinkling cheerfully. It lacked only the Christmas fairy on the top.

'We need somebody tall,' said Sister, looking round the little group of staff and visitors, 'to reach from the ladder without disturbing the other decorations.'

'Will I do, Sister?' said a deep voice, and Nicholas strode up the ward, his brown hair looking a bit damp and dishevelled, his white, badge-covered coat flapping. 'I've only just managed to get away from Theatre, or I'd have been here earlier to offer my services.'

'Sure, and you'll do fine, Doctor,' said Sister O'Brien, looking very pleased. She handed him the little doll, freshly dressed by her each year in sparkling white. 'There you are; it just wants hooking over the topmost spike.'

'Right.'

They all watched as Nicholas climbed the stepladder, leaned carefully over the decorated branches, and hooked the fairy into position. A small cheer went up from the children and helpers. Somebody turned up the volume on the music system and a cheerful voice singing about the reindeer with the red nose swamped the ward. Everyone joined in singing, with Nicholas, at his calm best, very much at ease, conducting from halfway up the ladder.

Poppy's eyes filled with sudden tears as she gathered up one of the toddlers who was ambling round, wide-eyed and thumb in mouth, and hugged her tight as she sang along with the others. How appropriate, she thought, for Nicholas to be involved in a reindeer song.

She blinked through her tears, and saw that Nicholas was looking straight at her, a half-smile on his lips, and a tender expression in his eyes. He's remembering his chocolate reindeers too, she thought, and managed to give him a watery smile.

The song came to an end. Nicholas got down from the ladder, said a few words to Sister, and made for the door. He stopped as he drew level with Poppy, still holding the small child in her arms.

'Very appropriate, the reindeer song, don't you think?' he asked. His eyebrows were raised quizzically, but his eyes were still soft and tender and full of reflected golden lights from the tinselled tree. He tickled the small girl under her chin, and she gurgled with pleasure. 'Ah, innocence,' he murmured. 'Perhaps an undervalued gift, as we get older.' He moved closer to Poppy, and smiled down at her, touching her lightly on the arm. 'Madonna and child,' he whispered. 'It suits you wonderfully. With children is where you belong.'

He had gone before Poppy had time to recover from the sensation of warmth and euphoria that his closeness and his words caused. The little girl wriggled out of her arms and tottered towards the Christmas tree, where people were milling around piling presents on the platform, beneath the pine-scented branches. Poppy was still standing mesmerised and happy, and trying to take in what he had said to her, and the way he had said it, when Sister O'Brien reminded her that the medicine round was due.

It was then, standing in the middle of Peter Pan, that Poppy knew, absolutely for sure, that she was irrevocably in love with Nicholas Fordyce, remarkable as it seemed after knowing him for only a few weeks. Astonishingly, after her earlier doubts about his intentions, she was equally sure that he was at least half in love with her. She had felt it emanating from him. Why he held back must be because he still distrusted her, or someone who he thought had helped her up the career ladder. Never mind, she would be patient, and eventually convince him of her innocence. So great was her love for this man that she was sure that she had the strength to wait.

The next day, the twenty-third, was busy with children being discharged home for good, or for a Christmas break. The remaining children who could be moved were brought into the main ward, ready for the celebrations. The change in routine seemed to do them good; they were bubbling over with excitement, and their bravery over their various disabilities was quite tear-jerking.

Poppy performed all her duties with her usual tender, loving care and refused to be downcast on learning that Nicholas had the day off. It would have been wonderful if he had sought her out after the highly emotional encounter in the ward the previous afternoon, but she wasn't unduly disturbed by the fact that he hadn't. In time he would, her new-found confidence confirmed.

She was working till nine o'clock, and didn't get home till nearly ten. The phone rang as she let herself into the welcoming warmth of Victoria House. It was bitterly cold outside.

'I'll get it,' she called to Jacky and Ruth, who were in the kitchen.

She picked up the receiver. 'Hello,' she said, 'this is —— '

'I know who it is, my dear,' said Nicholas's deep

voice in her ear. 'I was hoping to catch you when you came off duty.'

Poppy's heart leapt, and the hairs on the back of her neck prickled. It was blissful to hear his voice. It was some moments before she could answer, and then she heard herself say inanely, 'Oh, why?' She held her breath, wondering what he was going to say.

Nichllas laughed. 'Very to the point,' he said. 'Two things really. One was to apologise for going rather over the top yesterday on the ward—you know, my Madonna and child remarks. Very emotive stuff, all due to the sentiments of the festive season. I hope that I didn't embarrass you.'

A shaft of bitter disappointment went through her. She hadn't known what she expected him to say, but it wasn't this, certainly not a retraction of those gentle, loving words. She felt voiceless, but pulled herself together, and said coolly, 'No, of course I wasn't embarrassed; as you say, it was all down to the Christmas spirit.'

'Oh, splendid,' he replied, and then added in sincere tones, 'I wouldn't want anything to spoil our friendship. We must get together again for a drink over the holiday; that is, when time and duty allow. Would you like that?'

Poppy kept her voice steady. 'I should like that very much. Now what was the second reason for phoning?'

He said in a teasing voice, 'Guess who I had lunch with today, while I was up in town?'

'I can't begin to guess.'

'Your father.'

'My father?' she squeaked in astonishment.

'Yes. He was lecturing at the symposium I attended

today, and invited me to his table afterwards. He actually remembered me as a raw young houseman. I was briefly on his team, but you knew that, didn't you, Poppy?' He was teasing still, daring her to deny that she had discussed him with her father.

Poppy swallowed, recalling her conversation with her father, into which she had casually introduced Nicholas's name. She wondered how her father might have relayed this to Nicholas, perhaps embroidering it a little, or by nuance suggesting some significant reason for his name being brought into the conversation.

'You know jolly well that I do,' she said brightly. 'Daddy's obviously been talking. Not that it matters, surely. I only wanted to find out how you knew whose daughter I was. You never said, you see, that night when you came to supper.'

'And dropped my bombsell.'

'Exactly.'

'You never asked, Poppy,' he said quietly. 'You were just angry with me for knowing who you were.'

'You never gave me a chance, and you were so defensive about Nina. Right up until today I thought that you still resented my getting the job on Peter Pan. You seemed to keep changing towards me.'

'No, I soon realised that you would not have traded on your father's reputation to improve your career prospects, but people are impressed by names and sometimes act differently. However there were — are — other reasons for our just remaining good friends.'

'Are you going to tell me about them?'

'Perhaps, but not now, Poppy, not over the phone;

it would take too long, and it's too complicated. One day, perhaps, when we know each other better.'

'Has it anything to do with my father?'

'Indirectly, maybe.' She heard him breathe in deeply, and then he said quite cheerfully, 'Well, Poppy, love, we'd better say goodnight now. We've both got a busy time ahead of us over Christmas, and an early start in the morning.'

'Yes, we have. Goodnight, Nicholas, see you in the morning.' She kept her voice steady and cheerful, refusing to be dismayed by what he had said. With a quiet certainty she knew that her love for him was too deep to be set aside for some unexplained reasons of conscience, and more firmly than ever she believed that he loved her too, whether he was aware of it or not.

Nicholas said quietly, 'Goodnight, Poppy, bless you, sleep well.'

Surprisingly, she did sleep well, and woke to a Christmas Eve world that had changed overnight. A thin powdering of snow lay over the landscape, not very deep, but crisp and even, she thought, as the tune of Good King Wenceslas filtered into her mind. Well, tonight she would be singing that old carol and many more, as, together with dozens of other staff, she visited every ward in the hospital to bring Christmas to the patients.

It was a tradition cherished at Princes Park, and, as per custom, all the nurses would reverse their old-fashioned cloaks, and wear the red side outside, and the male carol singers would carry lighted tapers, as they had done for many years.

Driving carefully to work over the freezing layer of snow, Poppy felt exhilarated. She was confident that whatever reservations Nicholas had would eventually be resolved; meanwhile, she would take pleasure in their friendship.

The day passed quickly, with all the usual ward work to be done for the children remaining over Christmas. There were still dressings to change, injections to be given, and medicines distributed. The houseman and the junior registrar were about from time to time, but of Nicholas there was no sign. He was apparently involved in Maternity and the special baby unit.

Poppy finished duty at six, and went off to the cloakroom to tidy up ready for the carol service, which was to start in Peter Pan at six-thirty. From past experience she knew that during the course of the evening staff coming off duty would join the carollers wherever they happened to be in the hospital. She was sure that Nicholas would arrive at some point, and hoped very much that it would be while they were still singing in Peter Pan.

By half-past six, about thirty people had collected in the corridor outside the ward. Poppy saw that they were headed, as on previous years, by the matron, Clare Dunn, and the medical director, Dr Gregory Hurst. They were both fine singers, and, at a signal from Matron, the Christmas choir began walking down the corridor to the ward, singing 'Away in a Manger' as they went. Inside the ward they grouped themselves about the tree, and in clusters round each bed, encouraging the children and the visitors who remained to join in the singing.

Poppy sang her heart out, for this year these children

were her children, and she wanted to make it up to them for being in hospital when they should have been at home with their families. She longed for Nicholas to be there, for she knew that he felt the same way about his small patients.

To her joy, he arrived as they were finishing 'Away in a Manger', and made his way down the ward to where she was sitting with a small girl moved in from the oncology ward.

Nicholas perched on the other side of the bed, and took the child's hand, and smiled down at her and then across the bed at Poppy. 'I promised Jennifer that I'd be with her for the carols,' he explained softly, 'if I could get away.' His eyes gleamed in the dimmed lights of the ward and the reflective glimmer from the Christmas tree. They were full of love, a wide, caring love that embraced his patients, Poppy thought, gazing into them, knowing, but not caring, that all her love for him must be showing in hers.

'Oh, I'm glad you could make it.'

She struggled not to be disappointed that he hadn't come to sit with her, and then felt incredibly mean as the little girl beamed at them both, and whispered, 'I am lucky to have Dr Nick and my favourite Nurse Poppy sitting on my bed.' She tucked her other hand into Poppy's, and sighed with contentment.

Matron announced that the next carol was to be the one that the children themselves had chosen, based on an old spiritual song.

'It tells the story of Mary and her baby boy,' said Matron, 'and some of the children have been practising to sing the first verse on their own.' Three children had grouped themselves beneath the tree. Matron turned and smiled at them. 'Now, at the count of three. . .' she said.

At first waveringly, and then more strongly as their confidence grew, the children's high treble voices rang out sweetly as they sang the time-honoured words about the birth of Jesus. Joyfully, everyone joined in the rousing, rhythmic chorus, and the rest of the carol. Jennifer, in spite of her frailty, joined in too, piping out the rousing words of praise, and shaking her head, sparsely covered with newly growing hair, in rhythm with the music.

Poppy felt tears stinging her eyes, and put an arm round the child's thin shoulders, just as Nicholas did the same. He squeezed Poppy's arm, and looked into her eyes. 'Emotional stuff,' he murmured.

'Yes,' she whispered. 'I can hardly bear it.'

'Yes, you can, for their sakes,' he said gruffly. 'They depend on us to be strong and cheerful.' He found her hand resting on Jennifer's shoulder, and pressed it. 'Don't go all soppy on them; let's have one of your famous smiles.'

Tremulously Poppy smiled at him.

'That's better,' he whispered, and her heart lurched as he returned her smile with a lop-sided one of his own.

The carol came to an end, amid much applause for the children. Everyone sang 'O Little Town of Bethlehem', and then the choir moved on to continue their tour of the hospital, leaving the staff on duty on Peter Pan to settle the excited children for the night.

To Poppy's intense pleasure, Nicholas took her small hand in his large one as the tour continued, and she walked beside him in a daze of delight, conscious of his warmth and strength.

Suddenly his bleeper sounded, and he went off to find out who wanted him. He didn't return, but even his absence failed to quell the fountain of happiness that continued to bubble inside her, a reminder of his warm, reassuring presence.

Christmas morning dawned greyly, with occasional snowflakes fluttering down and settling on the frozen surface left by yesterday's fall.

The ward was busy from the moment Poppy went on duty. All the usual chores had to be done for the children, and, as some of them were very ill, which was why they hadn't gone home for Christmas, these were often long, slow, painful processes.

As always, Poppy was astonished by the resilience and bravery of most of the children. Today they were bubbling over with excitment because it was Christmas Day. The tiny children were looking forward to the visit by Father Christmas, due to take place at midday. The older children, well primed by Sister O'Brien, had agreed to go along with the myth of Father Christmas coming from the North Pole, to please the little ones.

Poppy felt almost as much on tenterhooks as the children as twelve o'clock drew near, knowing that Nicholas would appear in a beard and a red and white cloak, drawing a sledge full of presents for the sick children.

He came on the dot of twelve, acting so well that the small children were convinced that he was the real thing, and even some of the older sceptics of nine and ten weren't quite certain about his identity.

The thought that some of these children wouldn't be around for the following Christmas brought a lump to Poppy's throat, and while Father Christmas was giving out the last of his presents she disappeared into the sluice-room.

A few minutes later, the door opened, and, without turning round, Poppy said apologetically, 'I'm sorry, I won't be a moment, Sister; I feel such a fool.'

'It can happen to the best of us,' said Nicholas's voice. 'You're just too tender-hearted; you'll have to toughen up a bit.'

Poppy spun round and stared at him. 'Oh, Nicholas,' she said, and stood uncertainly by the sluice sink. 'I will, I promise; it's just that ——'

'I know,' he said gently. 'It takes some getting used to.' He pulled off his beard and pushed the cowl of his cape back from his face, and shot back the red and white cuff to look at his watch. 'I'm on duty in a few minutes,' he said, 'until midnight, and there are several very sick babies. I'll not have a chance to wish you a happy Christmas later, so I'd better do it now.' He took a couple of strides into the sluice-room, and opened his arms. 'Come here,' he said in a firm voice, 'and let Father Christmas, or Dr Nick, if you prefer, give you a hearty festive kiss.'

Poppy knew that he was being jokey and kind to reassure her, but she would have preferred him to offer something more romantic than a hearty kiss.

She forced herself to say cheerfully, 'What, no mistletoe, Father Christmas? How remiss of you.'

'Oh, I think we can manage without,' Nicholas said easily. He put his arms round her and drew her close, and then kissed her on the mouth with warmth and gentleness, but without passion. He lifted his head and looked down on her. 'Happy Christmas, Poppy,' he said softly. He fished a small package out from beneath his cape. 'A little something,' he said, pressing the gaily wrapped parcel into her hand. 'With love from Saint Nicholas.'

He turned and left the sluice-room, and she heard his Father Christmas boots clumping away down the corridor.

CHAPTER TEN

THE first thing that Poppy saw when she opened her eyes on Boxing Day morning was Nicholas's Christmas present. She propped herself up on one elbow and gazed at the tiny oval picture of the Madonna and child in its silver frame. A wave of great happiness swamped her at the thought of Nicholas choosing this just for her, a reminder of his remark on the tree-decorating day, when she had held the toddler in her arms. It was a very special present, and surely conveyed a special message about the way in which their friendship might grow into something closer.

She hadn't been able to thank him, as she hadn't seen him after he left Peter Pan yesterday. There was a crisis in Maternity, where a woman had given birth to very poorly twin girls. She'd heard that Nicholas and the rest of the team had fought a life-and-death battle for hours, and were still fighting it when she had gone off duty to enjoy the rest of Christmas Day with her friends.

It was another cold morning, she discovered as she set off for work. There had been a further light fall of snow in the night, which sparkled on hedges and walls in the pale winter sunshine, though the snow on the road was beginning to turn to icy slush. A day for accidents, she thought sombrely, though even that awful thought couldn't dent her happiness in the knowledge that at some time during the day she would be seeing Nicholas.

In fact, she saw him as soon as she entered the corridor leading to the paediatric unit. He was coming towards her with his head down, shoulders hunched, hands in the pockets of his white coat, stethoscope hanging round his neck.

He became aware that someone was approaching, and looked up and saw her. For one unguarded moment his face lit up, then the shutters came down, and he looked at her with a cool, unsmiling expression. Poppy's heart sank. How could he look at her like that when only the day before he had given her the precious picture as a Christmas present?

She drew near, and saw that he was drawn and haggard from lack of sleep. She wanted to touch his lined cheek, and kiss his drooping, well shaped mouth, to let him know how much she cared, but the expression in his eyes warned her off. He wasn't in the mood for anything personal.

'How are the twins?' she asked, keeping her voice steady, professional.

'Hanging on,' he said laconically, 'just.'

'Oh, Nicholas, I am sorry.' She risked touching his arm.

He looked down at her hand and frowned. He said almost roughly, 'Yes, well, it goes with the territory, doesn't it? Mustn't get too involved.'

He raised his eyes and latched them on to hers, and for a moment they spoke volumes, and then they became dark and expressionless again. 'Well, I must push off, catch a couple of hours' sleep before returning to the battlefield.'

His voice was hard and bitter, disillusioned. Now was not the time to thank him for her present. He was obviously worried about the twins. Poppy swallowed her disappointment, and said quietly, 'Yes, you must get some sleep. Are you staying in the residency?'

He nodded.

'Well, I might see you later; I want to ——'

'Perhaps,' he said briskly, and began to walk away.

She felt as though he were piercing her heart with his coldness. He was deliberately locking her out. She shivered; she felt shocked. There was no sign of the gentle, loving man who had given her the silver-framed picture.

Nicholas turned back and stared at her from a few feet away. 'I wish things might have been different,' he said, 'and your father were not who he is. It makes everything very complicated. I'm sorry if I've given you cause to think. . .' He paused. 'And that present that I gave you, Poppy, don't think of it as anything significant. It was a spur-of-the-moment thing; I picked it up in a junk shop.'

He turned again and continued to walk away from her.

Poppy felt as if he had thrown a bucket of cold water over her. What did he mean about her father? What had that got to do with anything? She took a few deep breaths, and told herself that he didn't mean what he had said about the present he had given her. How could he? Every gesture he had made over the last few days, every word, had intimated that he regarded her as something special. He might have tried to fight it, but he hadn't succeeded. The looks that they had exchanged had spoken volumes. And the sexual glow and passion that had enveloped them when they had kissed beneath the mistletoe had to mean something. He might try to dismiss it, but it had happened.

He'd talked about her lack of sophistication and vulnerability, but increasingly she had felt that they were excuses that he had dreamed up to cover his real reasons for holding back, whatever they might be. Well, she wasn't going to let whatever it was that was bothering him stand in her way; she would be firm in her resolve to let time work its magic and bring them together. If he wanted to believe that she had got where she was through influence, let him. Clearly he still admired her father, though he seemed to think that he might have been instrumental in her securing the staff nurse's post on Peter Pan. He must think that it was all right for a father to support his daughter under any conditions, while objecting to the daughter taking advantage of her position. How very male, and chauvinistic! And yet she couldn't hold it against him.

She squared her shoulders, and lifted her head high, and felt her spirits rise with her determination. Showing a calm and cheerful face, she reported on duty to Sister O'Brien.

Just after dinners had been served, news began to filter through that there had been a bad accident on the motorway. They heard that a coachload of children from the local care home had been in collision with an articulated lorry, and that many children were badly injured.

By two o'clock, ambulances began to stream into Casualty, carrying large numbers of injured children. Peter Pan were warned to expect admissions. By three o'clock the maintenance team had dismantled the

Christmas tree in the main ward to make room for more beds, and empty beds were prepared to receive the casualties.

The first of the patients arrived: a little girl, concussed, and with her face cut by glass. She needed dressings to the wounds, and was to be monitored quarter-hourly for pulse and blood-pressure, and nursed in a darkened cubicle at the end of the ward.

Within the next half-hour, more badly injured children were admitted, and the ward bustled quietly as nurses and doctors set up drips and pulleys, and tried to reassure frightened children.

Nicholas came in at one point, still in theatre greens, to confer with his junior and advise about treatment for some of the more tricky cases. He stood at the end of a curtained bed where Poppy was doing observations on a small, sedated boy. It was a world away from their encounter that morning.

His tired, sombre eyes met Poppy's. 'Pretty grim, isn't it?' he said hollowly. 'All these poor kids — torn to pieces, some of them. They were on their way to a pantomime, you know.'

Poppy nodded, and whispered, 'It's worse because they're in-care children, and many of them are orphans, and there are no parents to be concerned about them.' Her voice faltered, and tears pricked at her eyes. She blinked and swallowed.

Nicholas stepped round the bed and gripped her shoulder with one hand, and turned her face towards him with the other. The curtains seemed like walls, isolating them from the rest of the ward. His eyes were great pools of darkness, deep, fathomless, his tender mouth only inches from hers. He kissed her gently.

Warmth, physical and emotional, radiated from him, reaching out, touching her.

'Don't cry, Poppy, I couldn't bear it,' he said gruffly. He dropped his hands, and stepped back. 'I've got to go. Be strong for me, please.'

He swished aside the curtain, and she heard his rubber-booted feet squeak away down the ward. I always seem to hear or see him walking away from me, thought Poppy sadly, and then, remembering his mouth, soft on hers a moment before, was comforted. Deep down she knew that he needed her as much as she needed him.

The memory of that kiss continued to comfort her over the following days, when life was one heavy slog on the full wards. Trained staff dispensed with days off, and worked long hours to cope with the volume of work. As the less injured children were discharged, their beds were taken up by young patients on the waiting-list.

On a day-to-day basis, Poppy had only fleeting glimpses of Nicholas. He was even busier than the nurses, with his work on the special baby unit, Maternity and Out-patients, and, of course, in Theatre. Now that the remaining accident children were out of danger, he had handed most of the routine work over to his juniors.

New Year's Eve came, and Poppy attended a party given by the medics in the residency, but she was not in a festive mood, and went only in the hope of seeing Nicholas, but of him there was no sign. Evidently he was still working somewhere in the hospital, and hadn't even found time to bring in the New Year — or, came the unwelcome thought, he was deliberately keeping his distance from her.

Everyone on the ward missed his particular brand of care and humour.

If it hadn't been for another Nicholas, Poppy thought, going on duty one wet January morning, Peter Pan would have seemed almost dull. That was an exaggeration, for she still loved her work, but she ached to hear Nicholas's lovely deep voice gently teasing the children and see his white, badge-covered coat flapping as he marched with long strides round the unit.

But the other Nicholas — young Nicholas — was a wonderful antidote to dullness or frustration. He was still recovering from injuries received in the accident, but was incredibly bright and brave. He was a great favourite with both staff and patients. In looks, thought Poppy fancifully, he might almost have been the older Nicholas's son, with his dark brown eyes, and wide, smiling mouth, and an untidy mop of hair swept back from his forehead. He was ten years old, but mature for his age. He had a talent for making friends with other children, especially the younger ones, and had the gift of dispensing happiness, which was all the more remarkable because his personal history was tragic. He had lost both his parents in a fire some years before, and had no other relatives.

'That young one is wise beyond his years,' said Sister O'Brien, when they were in the office discussing the report. 'Who would have thought that anyone could persuade young Timothy Ford to co-operate with his treatment, and get the Ford parents to see that they had to be firm with their son, for his own good? For sure I was getting nowhere with them fast, and yet young Nicholas managed it.'

'Yes, it was quite a breakthrough,' said the senior staff nurse. 'And one good thing has certainly come out of it: the Fords want Nicholas to go and stay with them at weekends when he goes back into care; with luck it will be a sort of home for him.'

'Now there's a lovely Christmas present for the lad to have, and no one deserves it more,' said Sister. 'Well, it's true enough that the Lord works in mysterious ways. Who would have thought that a dreadful accident could bring about one of God's little miracles and give our lovely young Nicholas a home?'

I wish, thought Poppy, as she left the office and made her way to the clinic-room, that God would work a little miracle for me and my Nicholas. If only he weren't so damned busy; if only we could talk once in a while; if only he'd tell me what's bugging him.

She started laying up a tray for removal of stitches. If we never have a chance to talk, her thoughts continued sadly, I'll never know what he meant when he made that strange remark about Daddy. She would wait forever for the answer if she had to, but her longing for Nicholas was beginning to be unbearable. There had been a dull ache in her chest ever since Boxing Day, when Nicholas had virtually rejected her, and had described his present to her as junk. That had hurt, and still hurt. And yet he'd reached out to her again when he'd kissed her with such sensitivity in the cubicle by the sedated child's bed later that day. She had thought then. . .

She bowed her head. 'Oh, Nicholas, if only I could talk to you,' she said out loud in an anguished voice.

There was a movement in the doorway, and she lifted her head to see Nicholas standing there, looking tall, and thin, and tired.

'I'm sorry,' he said in a low voice. 'I didn't mean to butt in. I'm looking for Sister; she isn't in her office.'

Poppy felt quite faint for a moment, seeing him standing there. Her heart thumped painfully. Had he heard what she had said? She swallowed a lump in her throat. She wanted to go to him and lay her head on his chest, and feel his warm body against hers. More than that, she wanted him to wrap his hard, muscled arms around her, and crush her to him as he had under the mistletoe.

She squashed her thoughts. 'Can I help?' she asked in a professionally correct voice. 'Sister's at a meeting.'

Nicholas stared at her for a moment, almost seeming to look through her. 'No, it's all right. I just wanted to see the children who are for discharge tomorrow. You carry on; I'll go through to the ward, if I may.' He made his voice flat and toneless, ungiving.

'Yes, please do,' she said, as protocol demanded. 'The children will be pleased to see you; they've missed having you about.' Tongue in cheek, and hoping that he would understand that she had missed him, she added, 'We thought that you had been avoiding us.'

This brought a glimmer of a smile which failed to reach his eyes. 'I've been busy,' he said briskly, 'and still am. I must be off.' He turned away.

Poppy thought, I can't let him walk away from me again. She said in a small, trembling voice, 'Nicholas, wait; oh, please wait. We've got to talk. Please let's meet; you must have some time off.' She walked towards him as he paused in the doorway, and stood directly in front of him.

He looked down at her with dark, unfathomable eyes. 'All right, we will talk. When are you off tonight?'

'At eight, but it's Twelfth Night and I promised Sister that I would dismantle the crib and the decorations in the play-room before I go off. I should be finished by half-past eight.'

'OK, I'll pick you up in Reception then and we'll go somewhere for a drink and a chat,' he said in unemotional voice.

He turned and strode away, and this time Poppy didn't try to stop him.

Poppy got off duty sharp at eight and went through to the play-room, which seemed uncannily quiet now that the children were all tucked up in bed.

A wave of sadness washed over her as she removed the wall pictures, cards and paper chains that her little patients had made, and packed them away with the tiny tinsel trees that decorated each windowsill. Christmas, with its message of peace and good will, was over for another year. Next year there would be another batch of sick children making cut-out angels and painting unlikely reindeers.

'And where will any of us be next Christmas?' she wondered out loud, thinking of Nicholas, and all the young patients. 'Where will I be?'

'At a guess, somewhere with children who are in need of care and love,' said Nicholas. 'I told you before that you and children go together.'

It was unbelievable; he had overheard her talking to

herself again. It was almost as if he was meant to, Poppy thought wildly.

He was standing just inside the door of the play-room, as he had stood earlier in the day in the clinic-room, but there was something different about him now. It wasn't just that he was wearing a cream turtle-necked sweater instead of his badge-covered coat; it was something to do with his tone of voice, his attitude.

Her heart gave a little leap of joy as she realised that he was less cold, less hostile. It might not be significant, or alter what he had to say to her, but it was a start.

She said, matter-of-factly, 'I've nearly finished here. We did say half-past in Reception, didn't we?'

'We did indeed, but I finished earlier than I thought. Do you want a hand?'

'You could pack these wrapped figures into the box.'

'Right.' He moved across the room and stood beside her at the table, and began placing the crib pieces carefully in the box.

Poppy continued with her wrapping. Except for the small rustling sounds that they were making, there was absolute silence in the play-room. The air crackled with their unspoken thoughts. They were intensely aware of each other. They were being drawn together as if by a magnet. Instinctively they turned, but still they didn't physically touch; they just stood looking at each other, their eyes locked together in some word-less, mysterious fashion.

Nicholas broke the silence at last. He cleared his throat, and it sounded unnaturally loud. Poppy jumped, took in a deep, painful breath, and moved a few steps backwards. Nicholas reached out and took hold of her hands and pulled her gently towards him.

'Poppy,' he said in a low but firm voice, 'come here.' He let go of her hands and held his arms wide. She stood rooted to the spot. 'Come,' he repeated.

Like an automaton she moved forward and his arms folded around her. She felt warm, comforted, and raised her head. His eyes searched her lifted face. She thought he might kiss her, but he didn't, though their bodies were locked hard together.

'We've been foolish,' he said quietly, 'not to acknowledge the inevitable.'

'The inevitable?'

He gave a low-pitched laugh. 'Yes, this love-at-first-sight syndrome, which I was hell-bent on ignoring, because it didn't fit in with what I thought about you.'

She couldn't believe what she was hearing. 'Are you saying that you love me?'

'Well, of course.' His arms tightened round her. 'Surely you knew? It happened the moment that I met you at Peter Pan.'

'You looked as if you hated me, and later I thought it was because you were in love with Nina, and resented my getting the children's job, and then it turned out that you thought I'd got the job through my father. But that was all settled weeks ago. It's since then that you've behaved so oddly; some days so friendly — more than friendly — and some days seeming to hate me.' She swallowed her tears. 'I've been so, so miserable,' she said in a choked voice.

'Oh, Poppy, what the hell have I done to you? All on account of not wanting to hurt you, and my stupid pride.'

'Pride? I don't understand.'

'My dear girl, I know about your affair with that rotter Franks, your father's one-time registrar, and how he used you. I had also been involved in the nepotism game, hospital politics and all that, and felt overlooked because of it. But then I saw that you too were vulnerable, and I couldn't risk hurting you again by revealing my love, and have you perhaps think that I was doing what Franks had done. And my pride made me chary of putting myself in a position where I might seem to be looking for favours from your father. I decided that it would be better to get my consultancy first on my own merit, and then our relationship might stand a chance. What I hadn't reckoned with, my love, was how hard it would be to see you and not be able to declare myself.' He dropped a kiss on her forehead. 'I want to protect you, care for you, not hurt you.'

'So what's happened to make you change your mind tonight, Nicholas? Why are you telling me all this now?' She strove to remain cool and in control of herself. She must be sure of his love for her; there must be no room for future doubts. She had lived in the shadow of her famous father all her life, and knew how difficult it was to achieve anything without seeming to use him, so she could appreciate how Nicholas had felt. Well, pride was important, but not as important as love.

He smiled down at her, his strong face tender. He seemed to read her thoughts. He said quietly, 'A combination of things put matters in perspective, and made me see that love — any true love — is what matters most. Peter Pan at all times oozes with practical love, but it has been especially poignant over this

Christmas, and the children seem to be aware of it. Something that one of the kids said brought my feelings into focus. Young Nicholas, my namesake, came out with a theory about Christmas, and its message of peace and love and good will, that seems relevant.'

'That sounds like Nicholas junior; he's a great philosopher.'

Nicholas nodded. 'Quite,' he said. 'Well, he thinks that all the good bits about Christmas don't have to end on Twelfth Night; they can go on forever. I found myself agreeing with him. It didn't matter that he was referring to love in its broadest sense; to me it was just as relevant to the love that I have for you, which grows stronger every day. To hell with pride and caution, I thought, listening to this child spouting his words of wisdom. Go and tell Poppy that you love her; don't prevaricate further.' He crushed her closer. 'And that, my dear love, is what I am doing.'

Poppy's heart was banging away so hard that she thought that Nicholas would hear it. Nothing seemed quite real; she seemed to be floating, as in a dream. The play-room was utterly quiet as she and Nicholas stared and stared at each other. She felt as if she were drowning in the brown, bottomless depths of his eyes.

She moistened her lips with her tongue. 'You're not afraid of your pride being hurt?' she asked. 'Some people still might think that you're getting to my father through me.'

'My dear, darling girl, I don't care a damn what anyone else thinks, as long as you know that I love you because you are you, not because you are the daughter of Sir Rowland Pope. That's all that matters.'

He bent his head and trailed a feather-light kiss across her forehead.

Poppy shivered with pleasure. 'We don't know each other very well,' she said, trying hard to be practical.

'We've a lifetime ahead to find out,' said Nicholas. 'And I know all that I want to know about you for starters.' He dropped kisses on her eyelids. 'All I want to do from now on is look after you, my dear innocent and vulnerable Poppy. You won't be hurt any more. I'll love you, Staff Nurse Pope, forever and a day, as all the best love-songs say.'

His teasing words made her smile, and dizzy with happiness. It was wonderful to know that after all the ups and downs of the past weeks they were in complete accord, and love had won over pride.

'Well, you know, Dr Nick,' she teased back, 'innocent or not, I'll show you a thing or two when it comes to making mad, passionate love.'

Nicholas tightened his arms round her even harder. He said, suddenly serious, ' I don't doubt it for one moment; taken all round, you're good at this love business.' He looked round the play-room at the huddle of soft toys and the fluttering mobiles. He said, 'You do realise, Poppy, that you will have to share me with your small patients when you marry me.' His voice was deep and serious. 'Though you can expect the lion's share.'

Poppy whispered in an awed voice, 'You're asking me to marry you, Nicholas?'

'Yes, I am.'

'But we've only known each other for a few weeks.'

'What's time got to do with it if we love each other?'

'Why, nothing,' she said in a small voice, discovering

an amazing truth. 'Absolutely nothing.' She stood on tiptoe and brought her face close to his. 'Nicholas,' she said softly, 'kiss me properly, please, the way you did under the mistletoe before Christmas.'

'Are you saying yes to marrying me?'

'Yes, please.'

'Right, come here, woman.' His arms, already holding her close, moulded her body to his, and his mouth took possession of hers.

They stayed locked together for unmeasured minutes, until Poppy, breathless and trembling, drew back a little. 'You know,' she said in a whisper, 'Christmas can last forever if you work at it.'

'Let's work at it,' said Nicholas, and kissed her again in the quiet, familiar surroundings of the Peter Pan play-room.

Six weeks later they were married in the hospital chapel. Sir Rowland, 'once more on view', as he put it, escorted a radiantly happy Poppy up the aisle on his arm to join a distinguished-looking Nicholas at the altar rails.

The chapel was filled with their friends and colleagues, and, to their surprise, some of the recently discharged young patients with their grateful parents, including young Nicholas with his adopted family. As they left the chapel, a small girl presented them with a silver horseshoe and a card from the patients on Peter Pan ward.

They looked at the card, which was hand-made by the children, while they were waiting for the guests to arrive at the reception in the refectory. The picture on the front depicted Nicholas in his badge-covered white coat, over a colourful smart suit, standing next to Poppy, who was in uniform, but wearing a veil instead of a cap. Inside, bright, blotty letters spelled out the message, 'To Dr Nick and Mrs Dr Nick, with love from all on Peter Pan', followed by a scrawling column of signatures and crosses.

'I shall treasure it forever,' said Poppy, her eyes misty with tears.

'We'll frame it,' said Nicholas. 'It'll be a reminder in years to come of all the good things that happened to us during our first Christmas on Peter Pan.'

'What a brilliant idea.'

'Oh, I'm full of good ideas,' said Nicholas, a wicked gleam in his dark brown eyes, 'and the best idea was marrying you.'

He bent his head and dropped a kiss on her nose. 'That,' he said as their guests began arriving, 'is to be going on with.'

'Thank you,' murmured Poppy, deceptively demure. 'I look forward to the balance later, Doctor.'

'The rest of the prescription to follow,' muttered Nicholas, and he turned to greet their first guests.

Discover the thrill of *Love on Call*
with 4 FREE Romances

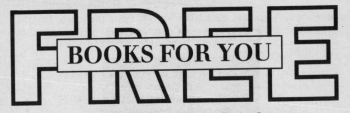

FREE
BOOKS FOR YOU

In the exciting world of modern medicine, the emotions of true love acquire an added poignancy. Now you can experience these gripping stories of passion and pain, heartbreak and happiness - with Mills & Boon absolutely FREE! AND look forward to a regular supply of *Love on Call* delivered direct to your door.

❦ ❦ ❦

Turn the page for details of how to claim 4 FREE books AND 2 FREE gifts!

An irresistible offer from Mills & Boon

Here's a very special offer from Mills & Boon for you to become a regular reader of *Love on Call*. And we'd like to welcome you with 4 books, a cuddly teddy bear and a special mystery gift - absolutely FREE and without obligation!

Then, every month look forward to receiving 4 brand new *Love on Call* romances delivered direct to your door for only £1.80 each. Postage and packing is FREE! Plus a FREE Newsletter featuring authors, competitions, special offers and lots more...

This invitation comes with no strings attached. You may cancel or suspend your subscription at any time and still keep your FREE books and gifts.

It's so easy. Send no money now but simply complete the coupon below and return it today to:

Mills & Boon Reader Service, FREEPOST, PO Box 236, Croydon, Surrey CR9 9EL.

--- **NO STAMP NEEDED** --- ✂

YES! Please rush me 4 FREE *Love on Call* books and 2 FREE gifts! Please also reserve me a Reader Service subscription. If I decide to subscribe, I can look forward to receiving 4 brand new *Love on Call* books for only £7.20 every month - postage and packing FREE. If I choose not to subscribe, I shall write to you within 10 days and still keep the FREE books and gifts. I may cancel or suspend my subscription at any time simply be writing to you. I am over 18 years of age.

Please write in BLOCK CAPITALS

Ms/Mrs/Miss/Mr _____ EP62D

Address _____

_____

_____ Postcode _____

Signature _____

Offer closes 31st March 1994. The right is reserved to refuse an application and change the terms of this offer. One application per household. Offer not valid to current Love on Call subscribers. Offer valid only in UK and Eire. Overseas readers please write for details. Southern Africa write to IBS, Private Bag, X3010, Randburg, 2125, South Africa. You may be mailed with offers from other reputable companies as a result of this application. Please tick box if you would prefer not to receive such offers. ☐

mps MAILING PREFERENCE SERVICE

ESCAPE INTO ANOTHER WORLD...

...With Temptation Dreamscape Romances

Two worlds collide in 3 very special Temptation titles, guaranteed to sweep you to the very edge of reality.

The timeless mysteries of reincarnation, telepathy and earthbound spirits clash with the modern lives and passions of ordinary men and women.

Available November 1993   Price £5.55

MILLS & BOON

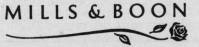

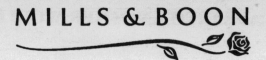

LOVE ON CALL

The books for enjoyment this month are:

SECOND THOUGHTS Caroline Anderson
CHRISTMAS IS FOREVER Margaret O'Neill
CURE FOR HEARTACHE Patricia Robertson
CELEBRITY VET Carol Wood

♥   ♥   ♥   ♥   ♥

Treats in store!

Watch next month for the following absorbing stories:

SURGEON'S DILEMMA Margaret Barker
A LOVING LEGACY Marion Lennox
FALSE IMPRESSIONS Laura MacDonald
NEVER PAST LOVING Margaret O'Neill